I Sell Love

LAWRENCE BLOCK
writing as Liz Crowley

CLASSIC EROTICA

21 Gay Street
Candy
Gigolo Johnny Wells
April North
Carla
A Strange Kind of Love
Campus Tramp
Community of Women
Born to be Bad
College for Sinners
Of Shame and Joy
A Woman Must Love
The Adulterers
Kept
The Twisted Ones
High School Sex Club
I Sell Love
69 Barrow Street
Four Lives at the Crossroads
Circle of Sinners
A Girl Called Honey
Sin Hellcat
So Willing

CLASSIC EROTICA #17

I SELL LOVE

A Night-by-Night Account of a Prostitute's Life
— By the Girl Who Lived It

Lawrence Block

"A Nice Girl Like You . . ."

I don't remember what he looked like. That's one of the bright sides of this business. After a while you don't remember faces any more. It's a good thing. They'd just keep turning up in dreams, or nightmares, and that's no fun. What I do remember about the joker is that he was putting his socks on inside out. It was kind of funny, in a way. He was in a great rush to get dressed, like he didn't want to be naked with me around now that he was finished.

"You know," he said, "you're a pretty nice girl."

I thought, *Here it comes.*

"A nice girl," he said. And then he delivered the line as though it was something that just occurred to him. It's a line you get from a trick at least once a week. Each one thinks he just hit on something pretty original. It's a pain in the neck, believe me.

"How did a nice girl like you get into a business like this?"

He picked the wrong day to ask. It was four in the morning, which meant I had time to squeeze in three more tricks if I hustled like a maniac. It was Wednesday night, which is always slow, and this particular Wednesday was slower than most. I didn't want to waste time feeding the joker a story. I just wanted to get rid of him.

"Did you get what you came for?" I asked.

He looked at me.

"You paid ten dollars," I told him. "Then I peeled off my clothes and we hit the sack. Did you get your ten bucks' worth?"

"Well," he said, "sure." His face got a little red.

"Then will you kindly tell me just what in hell you're wasting my time for? Time is money, honey. I've got work to do."

He got defensive. "I was just making conversation," he said. "I was just interested, that's all. You don't have to get mad at me."

I relaxed a little. "Time is money," I reminded him. "When I do something I get paid for it. A guy wants to take me to bed, he pays for it. A guy wants to hear the sad and tearful story of my life, he also pays for it. And I don't think you have the price."

"Take it easy—" He was heading for the door. It's amazing the way some tricks get embarrassed with a whore, like they're inferior or something. All he wanted now was to get the hell away. Already he was wishing he'd had the sense to keep his fat mouth shut.

"Go far away," I called after him. "And don't forget to turn your socks right side out. You look pretty stupid this way."

I waited for him to get lost. While I was waiting I straightened up the bed and changed the water in the basin on the dresser. I ran a comb through my hair and put on some fresh makeup. I hate like hell to plaster that pancake all over my face but it's part of the game. You have to let the tricks know what you are. Tricks are stupid that way. I honestly think a girl would double her business if she wore a signboard with her rates and the word *Whore* on it.

I looked into the mirror and it winked back at me. The dress was a red off-the-shoulder thing and I was glad I could still wear it. Too many girls can't. Needle marks. But my arms and shoulders were clear and clean, and my breasts raised hell with the front of the dress. There were little lines in the corners of my mouth but the tricks wouldn't notice them. They'd be too busy looking at the rest of me.

When my face looked nice and whorish I got out of the room and headed for the street again. It was a healthy walk. The rooming house I use for business is on 47th Street between Ninth and Tenth. The block for pick-ups is on Seventh Avenue between 49th and 50th. It used to be Eighth Avenue and probably will be again in a month or so. Pickup Alley changes its location every few months when one of the Citizens' Committees gets a burn on. Right now it's Seventh Avenue. I walked over and found a doorway to stand in.

For a few minutes I thought about the last trick, the one with a burning desire to learn all there was to learn about me. He got me pretty angry. They always want something for nothing. They pay for a roll in the hay and keep their eyes open for a little dividend. Some of them want to be loved. Others want to look inside your skin, like this one.

Well, if anybody wants anything from me he can damn well

pay for it. I don't give anything away, not a damned thing. I used to, long ago, but I know better now.

I remember thinking that anybody could have my story if he paid my price. It was something to joke about then. I didn't think it was going to happen.

I was wrong.

I'm telling my story right now. I don't have to pound the thing out on a typewriter. I just talk into this little machine here, and pretty soon somebody'll pick up the rolls of tape and have them typed up. The publishers of Monarch Books are paying me for it. It's a screwy deal but I'm not going to fight it. I found out fifteen years ago how this little world works. If you have something that somebody wants, you sell it to them. If somebody else has something you want, you pay for it. Up until now I only had one thing anybody ever wanted. Now I've got a story, which I hope some people will be interested in reading.

Not that money is my only reason for spilling this confession. Maybe I can help somebody by doing it. Looking back, I wish I'd had someone to warn me about what I was getting into . . . the heartaches, the abuse and the degradation. But I guess I'd better stop feeling sorry for myself and get on with it.

You might as well sit back and listen now. What the hell, you bought the book. And what you're reading here is straight goods.

*   *   *

First of all, I'm going to start off by telling you a few ways I did not get into the business. For one thing, I was not shanghaied by a gang of white slavers. Of course, there are girls who were conned into the business by a gang of hoods, but I wasn't one of them.

I didn't start swinging my tail around to support a narcotics habit, either. Plenty of hustlers do, don't get me wrong. You need big money to keep a junk habit rolling along. And there's big money in hustling.

But junk never happened to be my scene. I tried a pop once, years ago, but I didn't like it enough to spend the rest of my life nursing it along. I've poured a lot of gin down my throat, but that's something else again. I've smoked some marijuana now and then, but that also is something else. You don't get hooked on pot, except that too many girls get dissatisfied and go on to something stronger.

What it comes down to, I guess, is that I started turning tricks because I didn't know what else to do. That sounds wrong, but that's just the way it was. I became a prostitute because I had to make a buck and I've stuck with it for the same reason. Maybe I would have stepped out if I knew what else I could step into, but I couldn't see myself selling underwear behind a counter all day. And let's face it, outside of that, what else could I do?

But it could be better—a lot better. Every day it gets a little harder to look in the mirror. Every day the tricks take a little longer to make up their minds, and every day they make me a little sicker of myself and them. This is supposed to be a soft life with high pay. Yeah, the pay is high and the price *you* pay is higher, and I don't mean in money. Oh, well, I'm only thirty now. I've got a few years left before the sky falls in.

There'll come a day when the pancake makeup won't be there to make me look like a prostitute. It'll be there to make me look like a human being. I take good care of myself, so it'll be a while before I fall apart. I'll worry about it when it happens. In the meantime, I might as well make the most of what I've got.

Let me introduce myself properly. We never did go through that bit, did we? Well, to begin with, my name is Elizabeth Crowley. I'm thirty years old, as I think I mentioned. I live in a furnished apartment on West 73rd Street, near Central Park. I could save money by living where I work, on 47th Street, but I don't go for that sort of thing. I don't like to do business where I live.

I'm five-foot-five without heels and I weigh 133 pounds. I've got a pretty good shape. My legs wouldn't make Dietrich jealous but they're okay just the same. I wear a C-cup and what I put in it doesn't sag. Not yet.

I've got shoulder-length black hair and blue eyes. The eyes are a little near-sighted, but I don't wear glasses while I'm working. Can you picture a hustler wearing glasses? She'd starve to death.

Now you know who I am. The next thing is to tell you how it all started, and that isn't going to be as easy as I thought it would be. The reason is I don't exactly know where it all started. Maybe when I turned pro, which was thirteen years ago. Maybe when Jack Riordan raped me, which was two years before that. Yeah, I got raped. It sounds funny to think about it, a whore getting raped. It wasn't funny at the time.

Maybe it was before that. Maybe it started when I was born, or a little after that. You know, I get a bang out of that. I was born on 39th Street, just eight blocks away from where I'm working now. It was a lousy neighborhood then and it's not Park Avenue today.

They used to call it Hell's Kitchen. Maybe they still do. I used to swear I'd get the hell away from it. God, how I hated that neighborhood! And it's funny, because I never did shake it loose. It's that kind of neighborhood. An easy one to spend your whole life in.

In those days the neighborhood was Irish and Italian and Polish and Jewish. Each block was another country, and the kids from one block would line up and throw rocks at the kids from another block. Nowadays there are some Puerto Ricans mixed in with the rest, and they use knives and zip guns instead of rocks. But that's not much of a change. When I was a kid, the kids didn't use guns. But the countries didn't use hydrogen bombs either. Things change a lot on the surface but they don't really get a hell of a lot different.

Hell, I'm rambling all over the place. Once I get going, I've got one hell of a story. There's a rape in it, and a jail sentence. There's a pimp and a few crooked cops and a batch of whores like yours truly. I've lived a pretty interesting life. Don't worry—you'll get your money's worth.

But first I've got to get the show on the road. That's the hard part. Then the rest'll come easy. Let's see . . .

The hell with it. I'll begin at the beginning.

You Got to Start Somewheres . . .

I was born about nine months after the stock market crashed, in June of 1930. My old lady wanted me like she wanted an extra hole in her head, so I guess I was almost as much of a shock to her as the stock market crash was to a lot of bankers.

My mother was no worse than the other women in the neighborhood. My father was probably okay, too—whoever the hell he was. I say *probably* because Mom had a pretty good taste in men. She had a candy store on the corner of Tenth Avenue and 38th Street where she sold penny candy and an occasional pint of bootleg gin until Prohibition went out. She'd been married a few years before I came around but it didn't work. The guy she picked was a bum and he drank more gin than she sold. After a while she kicked him out. From then on there was always a man around the place, sometimes for a week, sometimes for a year or two. I guess I was lucky. Some kids don't have any father—I had dozens of them.

We had two rooms and a kitchen on 39th, a cold-water flat three flights up. The building was all rundown but Mom could have kept our apartment in better shape if she wanted to. But she was a pretty rotten housekeeper. She didn't like to wash dishes or make beds or clean floors. I can't blame her. I don't, either.

She was even worse at cooking. No matter what she brought home, by the time she finished boiling the hell out of it, it tasted like an old rubber boot. We ate most of our meals out, usually at a lunch counter around the corner.

Mom was Irish and so was everybody else on 39th Street. 38th Street was German and 37th Street was Jewish. Mom was Catholic, of course, but she didn't kill herself working at it. I remember going to Mass three or four times when she decided I needed religion. That was about all there was to it.

The neighborhood stank. But there were good sides to it. You grew up fast there, which was both good and bad. You had to grow up or you were lost. Take sex, for example. I knew what it was all about by the time I was nine years old. One night Mom brought home some big Polack longshoreman and the two of them were too stoned to bother closing the door. So I watched. They weren't too stoned to keep from having a good workout. It was an education, believe me. I learned a lot.

I learned something every place but in school. There was a law that said you had to go to school, but it was the Depression and the truant officers didn't bother stirring up too much trouble in Hell's Kitchen. They knew better. I went to school off and on for four or five years and then I said the devil with it. Mom didn't mind. She could use me to help out in the store during the day. I was ten or so, and that was old enough to sweep the place and run a few errands for her. They have laws against that, too, but they knew better than to try enforcing them. It would have been a waste of everybody's time.

Thinking back, it's hard to believe that I hated the place as much as I did. It was a ratty slum and I had a pretty lousy home, but we kids had fun—in our way. There was no television then and Mom's radio never got anything more exciting than static, but all of us kids had plenty to keep us busy. You could just sit out on the front stoop and something interesting would come along for you to watch—even if it was just a drunk staggering along.

One time a fairly important gangster got shot half a block from our house. I was outside when he got it, but it happened so fast I didn't see it until it was over. The guy came out of a liquor store with a package—it must have been a bottle, I guess—and a black car barreled around the corner. There was a loud rattling noise that made me spin around. Then I saw the car peel away and the man was holding onto his stomach. He fell over on his face and the blood started rushing out of him. We stood around staring at him. It was an hour before the cops got there and they never caught the guys who did it.

We knew who did it, of course. That was the thing about growing up in the Kitchen. We knew things the cops didn't know, and we knew what the rackets were about and how they worked. This one guy, for instance, was a Jew. The torpedoes were hired by the Italian mob from Little Italy that was moving into the West Side about that time. Maybe the cops knew this, too, but they never got the guys who shot the Jew. For that matter, they didn't get the Jews who shot down three Italians on Mulberry Street two days later. That was something I found out real early—the cops never got anybody important. Just the little people who didn't know how to stay out of trouble. The ones who had no pull.

From the time I quit school at ten until about thirteen, every day was pretty much the same. I got up about ten in the morning. Mom and I had breakfast around the corner and then went to the candy store and opened up for business. Most of the time I didn't have much to do. I just hung around and stuffed myself with candy, until Mom got an order over the phone. When that happened she would wrap up a package and tell me where to take it. Usually I got a tip. Most of the time it was a dime, but once in a while the package would be for somebody important, one of the racket people. Then I'd get as much as a buck. But that didn't happen very often.

Mom kept the store open after dinner but I didn't have to work any more. Then I'd find some of the kids and we'd sit around and talk or play stoopball or stickball. I remember a few of the kids. There was Mary Shea, my best girlfriend. Her father ran a tavern on Ninth Avenue and her mother was a lush. Maybe it was a good combination—at least that way the old lady got her booze at a good price.

Mary and I had a lot in common. It's funny, because we wound up different. She stayed in school longer than I did and later she got a job modeling sweaters in the garment district. It was the perfect job for her. Even when she was twelve, Mary was built like a bomb.

It's funny. I haven't seen Mary in a good fifteen years, maybe more. But I heard how she turned out. I met a guy I used to know and he mentioned he ran into her a year or two back. She married a small potato who worked the same place she did, a pants cutter or something, and the guy got out on his own and did pretty well. Now they've got a house in Scarsdale and a pair of kids and a lot of money.

The point is this—so many people blame everything on the neighborhood. You get the idea that everybody from Hell's Kitchen wound up either in jail or on the streets, and it isn't so. Mary had things as rough as I did and now she's sitting on her hands in Scarsdale. You can't stick the Kitchen with everything. It's a good bet that more whores grew up in the Kitchen than on Riverside Drive, but that's just part of it. There's more to it than that.

Even when Mary and I used to sit on the stoop and talk about how the neighborhood was a stinking hole, we both had different ideas on how to get out of it. Mary wanted to play everything legit. She figured if you worked hard and stayed honest, everything would break right for you. I had different ideas—probably because I had a chip on my shoulder. I was going to make it the easy way. None of this working hard for me. I knew some people who knocked themselves out and stayed honest and it got them nowhere.

Mary and I used to argue about it. You know the way kids argue, rambling all over the place. I had all the answers in those days and I was better at arguing than Mary. But she stuck to her guns. She never listened to me. I'm glad she didn't.

If I had a brain in my head maybe I would have listened to

her. Scarsdale's a lot nicer than West 47th Street. A husband's a lot nicer than a parade of mealy tricks. But little Liz was too sharp to listen to anybody.

I think I mentioned how I knew what sex was all about when I was nine. I kept learning. In any neighborhood kids find strange things in the gutters and alleys, and they were all over the Kitchen. Sometimes you would see a couple necking in a doorway late at night. Or if you went up on the roof during the hot summer, you could stumble over the bodies up there.

But there's a difference between learning what it's all about and finding how you fit into it. I don't mean losing your virginity. I mean having a pass tossed at you and thinking what it would be like and everything.

That happened when I was thirteen.

I was just starting to turn into a woman. My breasts had grown over the past year and another development had increased the business of the corner drugstore. But it took Jake Connors to clue me in, the louse.

Jake was one of my mother's mistakes. He was a thin, wiry guy who was busy playing house with my old lady. He must have been good at that because there was nothing else he was good for. He didn't work. He hung around the house reading detective magazines and guzzling beer while Mom kept the store going. Then the two of them disappeared into Mom's room and I would listen to the bedsprings jouncing until I got tired of it.

It happened one day when Mom was working and I was

home. Jake was home, too, and we were both in the same room. He was looking at me with a funny expression on his face.

"Liz," he said, "you're getting to be one hell of a pretty little chicken. You know that?"

I made some smart comment—I don't remember what it was—and he laughed. "C'mon over here," he said. "Come here and sit next to me."

I went and sat next to him. I wasn't too bright, I guess. I didn't know any better.

He needed a shave and a haircut. His hair was black, a crew cut that needed more crewing. His beard was sandpaper. He had a funny way of looking at a person, his eyes never staying still but flashing here and there. It gave me a funny feeling.

"Real pretty," he said. "Built nice, too. You're growing up, aren't you?"

He took hold of one of my breasts and began fondling it when he said this. He was a little guy but he had a big pair of hands. He gave a little squeeze and I didn't like it. It made me feel funny.

"Stop it, Jake," I told him.

He laughed. "I just want to touch," he said. "You'll like it, Liz. All I want is to touch you a little. Listen, kid—you be good to me and I'll be good to you."

I didn't like what he was doing but for some reason or other I didn't make him stop it. Maybe I was curious. And, in a way, what he was doing was sort of nice. I wasn't wearing a bra yet and I could feel everything he was doing. I felt myself getting warm all over.

"Let's take your blouse off," he said. "Let's see what you look like underneath, huh?"

"Jake—"

"C'mon," he said. "I just want to see. Be a good girl, Liz."

So I let him unbutton my blouse and take it off. It felt funny having a man look at me without it on. He had a wild look in his eyes and he couldn't keep his hands off me. First he touched my breasts and then he tried kissing them. I was scared now without knowing what I was scared of. But I didn't stop him because it felt too nice.

I tried to keep him from getting his hands under my skirt but he was too quick for me. That scared me stiff but it also got me even more excited. I think we would have gone all the way if Mom hadn't come home. I never would have been able to stop him. He was strong as a bull. Besides, I wasn't in the mood to put up much of a fight.

But then Mom came in and Jake never knew what hit him. Mom was a big woman and she knew how to throw a punch. She must have knocked him halfway across the room.

"Get dressed," she snapped at me. "Cover yourself."

Then she turned on Jake. "You snake," she yelled. "You mess around with her again and I'll get a knife and fix you so you'll never mess around with anybody!"

"Peggy—"

"Damn you, Jake! She's a kid. Can't you see she's only a kid?"

He was cringing now. He rubbed the side of his face where she slugged him. "You got a good punch, Peggy. But what do you want to fight with me for? We shouldn't be fighting, Peggy. We got better things to do."

"Jake—" Her voice was low and threatening.

"Can I help it if she looks so much like her mother that I can't keep my hands off her? C'mere, Peggy. We don't want to fight. Come here."

She went to him, still swearing at him and threatening him, but the sting was gone from her words. I watched while he kissed her and stroked her and led her into the bedroom. Then I sat there and listened to the Bedspring Symphony again.

Mom talked to me the next day. I guess the scene with Jake clued her in on the fact that I was old enough to get a lecture. I got one. She really laid it on the line.

"You keep away from Jake," she told me. "You keep away from men, period. And boys. They're only after one thing, Lizzie. They get that and that's all they want from you. You know what I'm talking about? You know what it is they're after?"

I nodded.

"You're only a virgin once," Mom said. "Then you give in and you're a tramp. If you want a good man to marry you, you've got to stay pure for him. Once you give in to one man, only the lousy ones want you. Your virginity's the most precious thing you got. You don't want to fool around and lose it. It's not the kind of thing you can grow back again."

She made me feel ashamed of myself. I felt like crying but I didn't. I never cried much, even when I was a little kid. I don't know why I didn't. It's just the way I was.

"A guy like Jake," she went on, "he was just fooling around. He looked at you and he liked the way you looked so he wanted to see what would happen. But if I hadn't come home I don't know what might have happened. It was Jake's fault for being a wise guy, sure. But it was your fault, too. You shouldn't have let him get anything started. A man gets started and he can't stop. You've got to stop him before he gets going. You understand what I'm talking about?"

I understood. I understood a lot of things. I understood that I was a woman and that I had something valuable. It made me feel good, knowing that. I never had anything valuable before. I felt important all of a sudden.

Jake stayed away from me after that. Mom must have really raised the roof because he hardly even said two words to me after that one time. A few weeks later he moved out for good. I was glad to see him go. Then Mom found herself another guy in a week or two, but this one left me alone.

Meanwhile, I started noticing things. I would look at the other girls on the street, the older ones, and I would try to figure out if they had done it or not. Some of the kids said you could tell just by looking at a girl's eyes. I would watch them and try to figure it out. It was interesting.

I got another pass a month or so later. I was taking a bottle of rotgut to a racket guy who was holed up on 38th Street in a real wreck of a rooming house. I knocked on the door the way Mom told me to, knocking twice, then waiting, then knocking three times. He opened the door and motioned me inside, then shut it quick.

He was a big Italian guy with a full head of hair and shiny teeth. He had a mustache that was trimmed nice but he looked like he hadn't shaved in the past few days. The first thing he did was open the bottle and take a good swig. He made a face, then capped the bottle and handed me five bucks for it. That's how much I was supposed to collect.

I thought I would have a tip coming but I didn't stick around to argue. I turned and headed for the door but he called me back. I figured a tip was coming so I turned around.

"What's your name, honey?"

"Liz Crowley."

He smiled. "You're a nice kid, Liz. Pretty girl. If you'll be nice to me I'll make it worth your while. How'd you like to make yourself ten bucks?"

Ten dollars! It was a lot of money. But I remembered what Mom said and I was scared stiff. I don't know why I said what I did but it turned out to be the right thing.

I said: "I'm only thirteen."

His eyes went wide and he stared. "My God!" he said. "You look older. You look sixteen, maybe seventeen. Or maybe I'm blind, I don't know. I'm sorry, Liz. I wouldn't have said that if I knew."

I wasn't afraid any more. He wasn't going to try anything. I believed him, because I knew racket people were always nice to kids. We learned that in the Kitchen, The crooks were aces-high, and the cops stank. That much was catechism.

"Look," he said. "I want you to do me a favor. You know a bar called the Silver Fox?"

I knew which one he meant.

"Go over there," he said, "and ask the bartender which girl is Margie. She's a redhead. Find her and tell her Vinnie wants to see her. She'll know who you mean and where I am. And here's something for you."

I took the bill he handed me and left without looking at it. Then I went to the Silver Fox and found the girl. I was halfway home before I remembered to look at the money.

It was five dollars. I decided right then and there that racket people were the best people in the world.

Always a First Time . . .

I wasn't the first girl Jack Riordan raped. And I wasn't the last, either. Rape in Hell's Kitchen was a little different from rape in the rest of the world. Most people think of a rapist as a guy with a couple of screws missing. In the Kitchen, a guy raped a girl because he wanted her and there was no other way to get her. You didn't call a guy like Riordan a pervert. You called him a dirty son of a bitch, but not a pervert.

Riordan was four years older than me and he stood well over six feet tall. He had what they call a barrel chest. His chin was like a rock and his arms were all muscle. He was a criminal at nineteen but strictly small time. The jobs he pulled were muscle jobs—stick-ups, beatings, that sort of thing. Rape was a sideline with him.

It was 1945. The war ended and so did my virginity. It wasn't an unusual occurrence for Riordan, but it made an impression on me. In more ways than one.

You know, they say no matter how many men you have you can always remember the first one. It's the truth. Even when the first one is a rape, you can remember every detail of it. I even remember what I was wearing, to give you an example.

It was fall, and I had on a yellow sweater, a black skirt and sneakers. I was fifteen and I should have been wearing a bra, but I didn't like them. So I was walking along, bobbling up and down a little, and the sun was down and the streets were getting dark, and there was Riordan.

He'd been trying to get to me for a long time. A month, anyway, which was a long time for Riordan to wait for anything. When he wanted something he took it. Me he wanted, but I'd been staying away from him.

This time I didn't have a chance. He had a load of beer in his guts and he wasn't stopping for anything. He grabbed hold of me before I knew what was happening and started hauling me off to the alley at the side of the building. I should have screamed then while we were still on the street. There was still time then. I didn't. Maybe I was too scared. Later on I got around to screaming but it didn't do any good. People are very careful not to notice anything in the Kitchen. They keep their noses clean.

"Get over here," he snapped. "I been waiting long enough."

"Please," I begged. "Please—"

He grabbed me. I tried to get away but his grip was too strong for me. He was a bull.

"You're gonna like it," he said. "You might as well like it. You're getting it just the same."

Riordan stank of beer and the alley stank of garbage. He gave me a shove and I landed on my tail. I knew what was coming but I couldn't even think about it. All I could think was that he was getting my skirt dirty. It was almost new and I didn't want him to ruin it. Isn't that a laugh?

The rest wasn't so funny. I was stupid. I tried to fight, and that wasn't too bright because I didn't have much chance of winning. I put up a battle, and the more I fought, the more I got slapped around. I got his face with my nails and he gave a yell. Then he hauled off and belted me one in the stomach and I thought I was going to break apart in the middle. I should have had the brains to quit then.

But all I could think of was that I had something valuable and that Riordan was trying to take it away from me. I clawed him again and he hit me in the belly. Then he banged my head against the ground and it hurt like hell. I couldn't even move while he got the sweater off and went to work on my breasts. He wasn't the gentle type. Maybe he was getting even with me for putting up a fight. Whatever it was, he squeezed and mauled my breasts until they ached.

If I wasn't afraid and if he wasn't so rough it wouldn't have been so bad. Every once in a while I got those feelings I had when Jake was fooling around with me. But I was so scared and he was so rough that the feelings got buried under the pain.

He got off my skirt and panties. I tried to keep my legs together but he was too strong for me. When he raped me I couldn't even think of it as something you could enjoy. It hurt so damned much. The pain was like a knife running straight through me. I waited for it to end and it wouldn't end and I thought I was going to die. It kept on hurting until finally it ended and he let go of me. I couldn't move. I just lay there while he looked at me and grinned. Then he got the hell out of the alley and left me lying there.

No cops came. They're only around when you don't want them. Nobody came at all. Fifteen minutes later I managed to get on my feet. I put my clothes back on but they weren't much good. The skirt was ruined and so was the sweater. And so, for that matter, was one Liz Crowley.

And you know, I didn't cry. Not a single goddamned tear, not before, not during and not after. I swore like a soldier and screamed like a baby, but I didn't cry.

I didn't tell Mom. I didn't have to because she figured it out just by looking at me. She'd have to be blind to miss it. I looked like something the cat didn't bother dragging in.

"You little bitch," she yelled. "You couldn't hang onto it, could you? You had to lead some guy on until he took it away from you. I thought you might turn out okay but not you. You had to make sure you'd wind up a tramp."

I didn't even bother to explain. I got raped so it was my fault. That's the way her mind worked. Hell, maybe she had something there. Maybe I should have carried a knife so I could cut Riordan's guts open. I walked around for days thinking how nice it would be to kill him. God knows he deserved it. I wanted to cut him up into little pieces and feed the pieces to a dog.

It wasn't enough for Riordan to rape me. He had to tell the

world about it. As soon as the world knew, Liz Crowley became a target. If a girl wasn't a virgin she was fair game. That
was the rule in the Kitchen. It didn't matter how you lost your
virginity. You could lose it riding a bicycle up a cobblestone
street—it was all the same. I was fair game. Period.

I didn't get raped again but I sure as hell got asked. Every-
where I went I felt eyes burning a hole in the back of my skirt.
Every boy on the street was trying to make me. Maybe some
girls could have kept away from them. I couldn't.

What the hell, I thought. You're a tramp now. You didn't
do anything, but suddenly you're a tramp. You got the name,
sweetheart. Now you might as well have the game.

It's not like I turned into a doormat. There are plenty of girls
who do and they make me sick. They run around after guys
and swing their tails nice and pretty and beg to be dragged
into the nearest alley. They act like the guys are doing them the
greatest favor in the world. I didn't get that way. I didn't want
the guys. I didn't want them at all. They wanted *me*.

Maybe I started hustling right then and there. Don't get
technical—I didn't make a dime out of it, not at the time. But
the way I looked at it was the same as I look at it now. They
wanted me, not the other way around. And they could have
me, but they were damn well going to pay for it. Not in money, because I was too thick in the head to ask for money at the
time. I got smarter later on.

They paid me in the way they talked to me and the way they
took me out. If I wanted to take in a show, all I had to do was
walk up to one of the neighborhood jokers and tell him to take

me. I didn't ask—I told. I got taken, too, because the jokers knew they'd get a damned good time out of the deal.

Occasionally I got some pleasure out of giving myself to these jokers, but it took time. At first, every slob was Riordan all over again, except that I wasn't putting up a fight. I would sort of lie there and wait for them to finish. Come to think of it, I must have been pretty green at the time. If I wasn't better than that now, I'd starve to death.

But then with one guy it was suddenly kind of nice. He was a pretty decent sort of a guy, which can make a big difference. He talked to me like I was a human being instead of something he was trying to get on the ground as soon as possible. It was the first time it was good and I remember it pretty well even now.

We went to a movie over on Eighth Avenue. The name of the picture was *A Sound of Distant Drums.* It was a Western and I always did like Westerns, especially when they get nice and rough. This one was nice and rough.

According to the program, the next step was the roof and a quick roll on the concrete. But Mike—that was his name, Mike Leary—took me out for a beer first. I didn't particularly like beer at the time but he took me to a nice place with soft lighting where the waiters wore matching suits. It impressed the hell out of me.

Mike was older than most of the others. He lived alone in a furnished room on Tenth Avenue over a cigar store that didn't make its money on cigar sales. I don't know how he made his dough. He never told me. We went up to his room and got undressed and went to bed. It was the first time I ever made love in a bed and the first time I had a chance to get all my clothes off. He wasn't in a hurry and he wasn't mean and he treated me like a person instead of a handy animal. This is corny, maybe, but the way he acted was more important than what we did. It made the difference.

He kissed me very gently. Then his hand found my breast and he was stroking me very tenderly. His hands were like silk.

"Relax, Liz," he murmured. "Relax, baby. I won't hurt you. I'll be gentle."

It went very slow and he kept touching me and kissing me. I felt something changing inside of me and pretty soon I was squirming all over the bed.

"That's right," he said. "That's my girl. It's going to be good, Liz."

And it was very good.

So for about a month I was in love. I moved out of Mom's place and moved in with Mike. I didn't have to work or anything. All Mike wanted was for me to be around when he wanted me. Not just in bed, but if he felt like drinking or talking or just going for a walk with me along for company. When we talked he didn't say a hell of a lot. He was what some people call Black Irish—clear blue eyes, jet black hair, a deep voice and a quiet way of talking. I don't know if he loved me or not. We never talked about it. But I loved the hell out of him.

When I was having one of my stupid periods I would wonder what it would be like to be married to him. Then I would smarten up and decide it couldn't happen. He'd be getting damaged goods. Men slept with girls like me but didn't marry them. The way I figured it, we would live together for a long time and then split up. I didn't bother thinking about what I'd do after he was gone. It wasn't nice to think about.

But he was gone in a month. Gone for good. A cop shot him twice in the chest and twice in the belly and he died right in the middle of the goddamned street. He didn't even have a gun. He was on a burglary job but he wasn't hurting anybody. He tried to run away. The cop didn't bother with warning shots. He gunned Mike down and let him die. He probably got a promotion.

Mom took me back after Mike was killed. She was mad as hell at me, but I was still her daughter. I moved back into my old room and started helping out at the store again. It seemed very strange, like moving back into another world. I was only with Mike for a month but it still seemed funny. Sometimes a month is a long time.

For a while I had a silly idea about staying true to Mike. Okay, it was stupid, but I was only a kid and I was pretty shook up at the time, both because of Mike and because of what was happening to my mother. She was going to hell. She was hitting the bottle more than ever and it was beginning to get her. Plenty of nights I would lay awake listening to her cough her guts out.

I blamed myself for Mike and Mom both. I had this jerk notion that if it hadn't been for me Mike would still have been alive. And I figured that Mom was drinking more because of me. So I sat around feeling horrible. You know—if sweet little Liz hadn't been a bad little girl, everything would be all right.

So I walked quietly through hell. There was nothing to do and no money to do it with. Mom worked two or three days a week and left the store closed the rest of the time. She stayed in her room with a bottle. Sometimes there was a man around to help her get loaded.

I tried to be a "good girl" but it didn't work. The only ones in the neighborhood who paid any attention to me were the boys who were trying to make me. Everybody else gave me a wide berth. I had the reputation for being "fast" and it stuck like glue. Going out for a walk meant getting passes or getting ignored. There was nothing in between. Staying home meant reading old movie magazines.

Talking to Mom didn't work. It was like talking to the sidewalk. Every day she got a little bit worse. I wanted her to see a doctor but she wouldn't go. It was about that time that I wished she hadn't lost her religion. The praying routine doesn't do much good as far as I'm concerned, but it helps some people. It would have been good for Mom. Anything to take the place of the bottle.

Now that I'm older I know a little more about what was wrong with her. It was a combination of things all working together to drag her into the mud. First of all, she was going through her change of life. This is enough to drag anybody down, but it was worse for a woman like Mom. The only thing that kept her flying right for years was men. Now she was too old for that. She felt she was no good for anything any more.

Then there was me. I blamed myself for what had happened to her and she blamed herself for what had happened to me. She knew she hadn't been much of a mother. When I went to live with Mike it knocked her for a loop. The way she looked at it, she was left with nothing. She was too old to hold a man and her only daughter was a tramp.

So she drank, and the drinking helped everything along. When she ran out of other things to feel rotten about, she felt rotten about drinking so much. She didn't eat and her health started to go. It's a pitiful thing to watch a big strong good-looking woman fall apart. There were times when she would hold long one-sided conversations with men she had known years ago. Other times she would talk to me, but it wasn't me she was talking to. It was me ten years ago. She acted as though I was her six-year-old daughter going out to play in the street. I answered her but she didn't hear a word I said.

Mike was dead and buried and my mother was on her way. It was only a matter of time before I gave up the idea of being a good girl and went back to the boys. What the hell else was I supposed to do? Go into a convent?

When Mom died it was the kicker. I was the one who found her on a Sunday morning after a long Saturday night that I spent in somebody's bed. I don't remember his name, but he wasn't the only one that night. He had friends.

It was quite a scene, believe me. There were six of them, and there was me. The guy only had the one room he lived in. You'd think the others might have had the decency to wait outside. They didn't.

I did it with one while the others stood around watching and making comments. Then the next one took his turn, and the next. After the parade was over they figured out some variations, so I could do it with more than one of them at a time. It was one hell of an evening. I didn't get much sleep. Plenty of bed, but not much sleep.

I came home and went into Mom's room to see how she was. Well, I saw, all right. She wasn't moving and when I touched her she felt like a dead fish. I looked at her and I got sick.

The men who came for her told me she must have been dead for a good ten hours. That meant I was tossing my tail around like a hopped-up rabbit while my own mother was lying dead in her bed. I felt pretty great.

I went to her funeral. It was the first and last funeral I ever went to. Some day I'll go to my own funeral, but at least I won't be alive for it. The luckiest person at the funeral is the dead one. It was the saddest thing in the world. I wouldn't go through something like that again for anything.

I saw them lower the coffin into the ground and I thought about dying. I tried to remember only the good things about Mom but there weren't so many to remember. I thought about the year she spent dying and I got sick again.

I wanted to cry. Even though I'd never had any real contact with Mom, she was always there, and somehow we were a family. Now here I was alone—with nobody in the whole wide world who belonged to me. I felt empty and completely hollow inside. I needed to cry but I couldn't. I don't know what it is about me that keeps me from crying, even when I want to.

You may have figured out that I wasn't the brightest kid in the world. I was a lot closer to being the stupidest. That's how I managed to get three months pregnant before I figured something was wrong.

I knew I couldn't have the kid. I had to have an abortion done, but I was scared stiff. You can get killed that way. But at the time it seemed the easy way. Since then I've heard stories about girls who got jobs done. A hell of a lot of girls died that way. I knew one girl who went to an abortionist. She's dead now. She didn't even die nicely. It took her four days to die, four days of pain and bleeding and agony. I was lucky.

So I went to Big Lucy. She was fat as a cow but she made a good living anyway. She was a prostitute who lived a few doors down the street from us. I didn't know her too well, just enough to say hello to. But everybody on the block knew she'd had a job done a few years back.

"No sweat," she told me. "There's a good little spade doctor uptown who'll take good care of you. Not one of these knife boys. He'll do a good job."

I was scared but I tried to keep from showing it.

"You got two yards? That's what he charges."

I didn't have a pot and I told her so.

"You're okay, Liz. I've got some money put by. I can lend it to you. But I don't make loans unless I'm getting it back. I don't hand out charity."

I told her I'd pay her back. She asked me how I was going to get the dough and I told her I didn't know.

"You know who the father is?"

I had to laugh. "All I know is he lives on the West Side. That doesn't narrow it down too much, does it?"

"I guess not. You've been a sap, Liz. You've been giving out one hell of a lot of free samples. A smart businesswoman you aren't. Now you're short on dough and you can't even figure out how to get hold of some. That's not too bright."

I knew what she was leading up to. It didn't sound good to me.

"Who got you in trouble, Liz?"

"I don't know."

"It was a man, you sap. So let 'em all pay for it. Hell, how dumb can you get?"

Sitting on a Goldmine ...

The abortion was less fun than a barrel of vipers. Big Lucy took me and we went in style. We took a cab up to the doctor's office, which was on 129th Street off Lenox Avenue. The neighborhood made the Kitchen look like Sutton Place. The doctor's office was on the fifth floor of a run-down tenement. It smelled of urine and disinfectant, and it reminded me more of a ladies' room in a cheap bar than anything else.

The abortionist was a short bandy-legged Negro with bright eyes and a neat goatee. He smiled, and I smiled, and Big Lucy handed him two hundred dollars in fives and tens. That was the extent of the preliminaries.

I lived through it. Let's leave it at that because it's not something I like to remember. The job was performed without benefit of anesthetic. It was not a picnic. It was almost a funeral. I lost too much blood, and I screamed blue murder, and I thought for several days that I was going to die. I came very close. Big Lucy took me home with her and let me stay in her bed while I tried to stay alive. She nursed me and she fed me, and for a week I stayed in that bed and wondered how much longer I was going to live.

Big Lucy pulled me through. I can still remember the way she would waddle over to the bed, bringing me something to eat, putting a cold cloth on my head to bring down my fever, sitting and talking to me.

"You're going to make it," she told me. "And then we're going to make a pro out of you. You've got the talent, Liz. I've done all right for myself, and I sure as hell don't have your looks. You've got it, kiddo. You're sitting on a gold mine."

That would get a smile out of me.

"I'm a big fat woman," she would say. "Fat as a pig. But a lot of men like it that way. They want to get all they can for their money. They like to swim in flesh. But you—you'll do better. You're young and you're built for action. You'll make a lot of money, sweetheart. You'll do real well."

I had to do well. I had to pay Big Lucy back. She was doing a lot for me. She was taking care of me and spending time with me. Mom was dead, and for the time being Big Lucy was taking her place. I'd have done anything for her.

He was my first customer. He was a skinny kid with glasses and pimples and I'll be damned if I know where Lucy found him. He wasn't much more than nineteen. Nineteen is old in the Kitchen, but this boy wasn't a Kitchen type. He was young and innocent and scared out of his wits. Lucy brought him into the room and then went out and closed the door. The poor trick looked as though he was waiting for the floor to open up and give him a place to hide. He kept looking around the room as if he was scared to look at me.

It made me feel funny, all motherly and grown up and everything. Before this all the boys were more experienced than I was. Now it was my turn to teach this guy what it was all about. I got a warm feeling out of it. Does that make sense? Here was this guy, so nervous he was ready to turn and run, and here was me, turning my first trick. And I felt motherly.

I was wearing a silk wrapper, a white thing with flowers on it. Lucy told me it was easier that way. She would bring the tricks in, and I would be wearing the wrapper, which would save time getting undressed. I opened the wrapper for a minute to give the trick a little excitement. Then I closed it and stood up.

"C'mere," I said. "You got the money?"

He walked over to me and handed me a bill. It was all crumpled up. I unfolded it and found out it was a twenty. Big Lucy knew how to pick them. I took the bill and put it in the bureau drawer.

Then I walked up to him and pressed myself against him. He was so nervous he was shaking. It wasn't hard to see he'd never had a woman before. He wanted me, and at the same time he was scared silly. I don't know what he was afraid of. Maybe he was scared that he wouldn't make the grade.

"I'm nice," I said to him. "See?" And I opened the wrapper so he could take a good look. He stared first at my breasts and then at my hips. He looked like he never saw a girl before.

"Take your clothes off," I suggested. He didn't move, so I

gave him a hand. I unbuttoned his shirt and slipped it over his shoulders. Then I took all his clothes off. He seemed very embarrassed when he was naked, so I took my wrapper off and threw it over a chair. We were both naked then and it seemed to put him at ease a little.

I led him to the bed and we stretched out together. The funny part of it was that I felt myself starting to get excited. Maybe it was because he was a virgin and it was my first time as a pro. It sounds silly, but it got me excited.

He got very interested in my breasts, touching them and feeling them, and that got me excited. The more he touched me, the more excited I got, and finally I found myself really wanting him. The money had nothing to do with it. His hair was blond and he was thin and nervous and I wanted him. Period.

But nothing was happening.

"I . . . can't," he said. He looked like he was ready to start bawling.

"Of course you can."

"No, I can't."

I forced a smile. "It's the first time, isn't it?"

He nodded, ashamed.

"Just relax," I told him. "Just be calm and relax. Everything's going to be all right. Don't worry about a thing."

He relaxed and I stroked his chest and rubbed myself against him. He pressed his mouth to my breasts and started kissing me. Then those hot little hands of his found some other spots to get interested in and I was going out of my mind.

Then he was all right, and I pulled him closer and showed him what to do.

I should have sent him home. But it was his first time and I wanted it to be good for him. I didn't let him go. I made him stay by me in the bed and I caressed his body and kept kissing him and pretty soon he was ready again.

This time it was better. Better for both of us. He was a man this time instead of a boy, and the world went around and around and exploded on top of us with one hell of a noise.

Then it was over.

He stood up, and now he wasn't ashamed any more. He put on his clothes while I stayed on the bed, my heart going a mile a minute and my eyes shining. Then he was gone, and all I could think of was how he was a man now and I was responsible.

When Big Lucy came back and I told her about it she said how I was a sucker to let him have me a second time without charging him. But I didn't feel like a sucker.

That was the good time, but the times after that were different. Now it was all business. Lucy would go to the bar where she always stayed—a hustler's bar where other guys steered the marks who were looking for women. Lucy would tell the tricks about me, and take them up to my room, and they would give me the money and then we would tumble into the bed. Liz Crowley, this is your life. Horizontally.

I was what is known as an "outlaw broad." That means a girl without connections. I didn't have a pimp and I didn't work for an established combination. All I did was stay in Lucy's apartment and handle whatever she brought me. The volume varied and so did the price. There were days when I had two tricks and days when I had fifteen. There were tricks who paid five bucks and tricks who paid thirty. It was a very changeable sort of a scene.

Some people might say that Big Lucy took me. The first two hundred bucks I made went to her, and after that she took an even half of my pay. As far as I was concerned, this was more than legit. Look at it this way—I was living in her pad without paying any rent, and she was doing the hustling. She could have taken all of it and I wouldn't have minded. All I was doing was turning the tricks. It was what I'd been doing for years without getting paid for it. Now I was getting paid, and I was eating good, and I was living high. I didn't begrudge Lucy a nickel.

I suppose the scene with the first one—the pimply guy who never had a woman before—stuck in my mind because it was so different with all the others. Most of the guys knew what they wanted and how to go about it, but they didn't arouse any feeling in me, motherly or otherwise. Most of the time it was bad. Not horrible. Just flat and uninteresting and horribly dull.

There were men who wanted me to do things that I didn't want to do. When I started, I figured that men just wanted to make love in the usual fashion. Then I got a guy who turned out to be married. That didn't make any sense to me at the time, which may go to show how young and stupid I was. The way I figured it, if a guy had a wife to sleep with, what did he want with a prostitute?

That's not the way it worked out. The guy laughed when I lay down on my back. "I don't want it that way," he told me. "I could get that much from my wife. If I'm paying for it, then I want something special. Not the regular routine. Something different."

I asked him what he meant. And he told me. He used words I can't use in print. Dirty words. They made me sick.

But I was just a whore. I couldn't argue with him. He was the man with the money. He was paying the bills. The things he had in mind may have made me sick, but he was giving the orders and all I could do was follow them. I did what he wanted.

I asked Big Lucy about it later. "Why don't they just want to make it?" I wanted to know. "Why do they have to dream up something different?"

Lucy didn't even raise an eyebrow. She just laughed. You could tell her experience covered everything.

"They're stupid men," she told me. "They're married and they suddenly realize they're not getting as much kick out of making it as they used to. They're bored with the same old routine. They think of another way and they figure that it's dirty, something their wives wouldn't do, so they find a pro."

A pro.

Like me.

*   *   *

There was another kind of trick, and he was the kind of trick I felt sorry for. Unmarried, not a pervert, not a virgin. A guy who slept with me because I was his only sexual outlet. There were a lot of them like that. They were the easiest kind of trick to handle, but I felt sorry for them. I thought about them needing a woman and not having a woman to make love to, and all I could think of was how unlucky they were. They didn't have anybody—not a wife or even a mistress. They were alone, completely alone. All they had was me.

New York was filled with men like that in the late Forties. Men who had gone to war, who had fought the Germans and the Japs, and who had come home to a strange world. They put in eight hours a day at their jobs and when the eight hours were up all that was left was love and sleep. They divided their time between work and prostitutes like me. I guess they were too self-centered to get married. At first I used to feel sorry for them. Then I began to think of them as just guys with a buck. That's the big thing about being a pro—you learn to accept everything and everybody. And, after a while, it gets easy. At first I did too much thinking, and thinking is dangerous. But I learned not to think. I learned to do my job on Big Lucy's bed. It was a hell of a lot easier that way, without thoughts to bother me.

"You're doing fine," Lucy would tell me. "The kind of hustling you've been doing is real good stuff. Pretty soon you'll be ready for a step up. I'm not going to try to hold you, Liz.

When you're ready to move I'll give you a hand. I don't want to keep you down."

I didn't know what she meant. I didn't know how complex the profession was. I didn't think of what I was doing as a step on a huge ladder. As far as I was concerned, my life was very simple. I was set. I would hustle right there in the Kitchen forever. That was all there was to it.

Big Lucy straightened me out. "You're young," she told me. "Now you get ten bucks a trick. Sometimes you get twenty and other times you get five, but the average trick pays about ten. That's not bad dough for a few minutes work. But you could get busted and thrown into jail any day. That's no good. You'd do a lot better in a setup where nobody could arrest you. And you'd make better money."

I listened to Big Lucy. She knew what she was talking about. If she could set me up in a better spot, I was all for it. If she knew a way for me to make more money with less risk, I wasn't about to argue with her.

"Hustling is tough," she told me. "Walking the streets can be hell on wheels. Getting arrested is pure murder. You don't want it."

That was the understatement of the twentieth century.

"Besides," she went on, "suppose you could live in a real swank place. Wall-to-wall carpets and posh furniture. A nice room and good food. Wouldn't that be better than this trap?"

I remembered the layout in a movie I saw once—a Park Avenue apartment. I thought about how nice it would be to live in a place like that.

"I'll set it up," Big Lucy said. "You've paid me back with interest and it's time you got a break. I'll set you up with Mamie Donner. You can't ask for better than that."

DOMESTIC EMPLOYMENT...

Mamie Donner was as unlike her name as it was possible for a woman to be. I expected a big woman, not as huge as Big Lucy but built somewhat along those lines. Mamie was just the opposite. She was all of five feet tall in heels and she weighed ninety pounds wringing wet. She had curly brown hair and trim ankles and a quiet way of speaking. But when she talked everybody listened.

"You work eight hours," she told me. "You have your own room that you turn tricks in. You might as well keep it clean, because you have to live in it. You start work at ten in the evening and you quit at six in the morning. You get your meals here. I don't care what you do in your off hours. Just don't get arrested. If you got a pimp, I don't want to see him. This is a class house. Pimps don't add to the class. Keep yourself clean and keep the place clean. That's all I ask. I'm an easy woman to get along with."

She wasn't lying. The house was classy, one of the few genuine houses left in New York after the war. It was on 95th Street off Broadway, a huge old private home that had been converted into what the books call a house of ill repute. When you come right down to it, there was nothing very ill about the house's repute. It was known throughout the city as a clean house with good-looking girls in it. Nobody ever picked up a disease in Mamie Donner's place. She ran a good establishment and she took care of her girls. We were grateful to her for that.

I was one of her girls. And working at Mamie's was like having a steady job. I didn't have to hustle. I didn't have to decide when I was going to work. Everything was decided for me ahead of time. I put in regular hours and I took on the tricks that were picked for me. It was like having a respectable job. Almost.

My room was nice—a big room with a good-sized closet and a nice mahogany chest of drawers. And, of course, a bed. It was the biggest bed I ever saw in my life. It was good for sleeping in and good for working on. We got along, that bed and I.

There were two shifts in Mamie's house, noon to ten and ten to six. I had the late shift, which was when most of the trade came in. The noon to ten crowd was lighter, mostly Madison Avenue types looking for a little matinee action. I was only eighteen and pretty good to look at, so I got the night shift. It was good work.

There was no haggling in Mamie's house. The price was a straight twenty no matter what you wanted or who you were. If a trick didn't have the twenty, Mamie didn't want his trade. She ran a good house and expected the customer to pay for it. And they paid. Through the nose.

We got to keep a quarter of what we earned. Out of a twenty-dollar trick, I made five dollars. It seems like a small percentage, but you have to remember that Mamie took care of room and board. And, of course, protection. While I worked at Mamie's I never had to worry about getting busted. An arrest can knock a girl for a loop. And Mamie's girls never got arrested. She really took care of us. We couldn't have gotten a better deal if we had a union.

There were ten of us, four on the early shift and six on the night shift. I never got to know the day shift girls, but I got fairly friendly with the ones on the night shift. Most of them were older than I was, but that didn't matter. We became pretty close.

Dotty was the Old Reliable. She'd been with Mamie for more years than she wanted to admit to and she must have been pushing forty, a big brunette with huge breasts and long legs. She was old for a prostitute, but she was proficient at her work and the customers didn't much care how old she was. She knew a lot of ways to get a man excited and she didn't care what she did. Usually a girl has certain scruples. There are some things nobody will do, some perversions that no prostitute will participate in. Dotty didn't draw lines. If the customer was willing to pay, she was willing to play.

Sally was younger. She was a one-way broad, which means that she would only make love in the most conventional manner. Mamie didn't like girls who drew lines like that but she tolerated it in Sally because she was so pretty. She was a real redhead, not the freckly type but a redhead with a peaches-and-cream complexion. She had an innocent face, too, which made her look younger than she was. I never liked her very much. She was snippy and always acted as though she was too good for the business. That didn't make sense to me. She was a whore the same as I was. She had no right to put on airs.

Honey was another redhead, sort of a chestnut shade. She was from Kentucky and I never did manage to figure out how she wound up in a New York house. Dotty told me once that Honey started out in a house in Newport, a city across the river from Cincinnati where anything goes. Honey was a nice kid, but it always seemed to me as though she didn't belong in the racket. Even her name was wrong for it. Honey was a nickname for Honour Mercy, which was her real name. And Honour Mercy is a hell of a name for a prostitute, if you ask me.

Kim was the boyish one. As Mamie put it, she appealed to the latent homosexuals. She was built like a boy, with narrow hips and hardly anything on top. Her black hair was cut in an Italian shortie haircut and she walked around like a man. She did good business. I found out later that she was a lesbian. She slept with men for a living and got her kicks from girls. I'll get around to that later on. There are lots of prostitutes like that.

Sandy was a blue-eyed blonde with the biggest breasts I ever saw in my life. She was a pretty girl, too, but she didn't stay at Mamie's very long. She was a junkie. She spent thirty dollars a day on heroin and if she didn't get her shot on time she would start climbing the walls. Sandy was a girl with no choice. She had to be a prostitute. There was no other way for her to earn the money to support her habit. Mamie hated hiring junkies, but she made an exception because Sandy was such a good-looking girl. When her habit got in the way, Mamie threw her out on her tail. I don't know what happened to her.

These were the girls I lived and worked with. For eight hours a day, seven days a week we turned tricks in that old mansion on 95th Street. These were my co-workers. They were nice people. The six of us kept that house jumping.

One rainy Thursday night, about two weeks after I had started working at Mamie's, I got into my first hassle with one of the girls. It's a funny thing but Thursday is sort of a medium night in a house, better than Monday or Tuesday or Wednesday, slower than Friday or Saturday or Sunday. This Thursday was a little slower than most because it was raining. There's something about the rain that cuts down a prostitute's business. I've never been able to figure out why.

Dotty and Kim were upstairs with tricks. The rest of us were downstairs in the parlor waiting for customers, with the exception of Sandy who was taking her monthly vacation those few days. The parlor was a big room with soft chairs and a fireplace.

Mamie brought this new guy in. He was tall and lanky, with a mop of black hair and an odd way of walking. He walked as though something was wrong with his left leg. It wasn't a limp exactly. The leg was just a little bit stiff in the knee. Mamie brought him in and pointed to a chair for him to sit in. He sat down.

"Pick whichever one you want," she told him.

"I thought I'd wait for Dotty."

Mamie grinned. "She's busy," she said. "She may be busy for quite a while. These girls are good, you know. Why not take one of them? They'll show you a good time."

Mamie went back into the front room and the guy sat there, looking nervously at Sally and Honey and me. It took him a long time to make up his mind and it made me pretty nervous. That's one thing about working in a house I never did get used to. When a trick stands around looking the different girls over and making up his mind, it always makes me feel as though I'm a slab of meat at a meat market. He looks at one and then another and you know damn well he's trying to decide who'll give him the best time. It makes me feel cheap. That's what I never liked about house work.

The trick was getting on my nerves. Finally I stood up and walked over to him. "Look," I said, "my name's Liz and I'm the hottest thing in the world. Why don't you and me go upstairs and I'll show you what it's all about?" I was pretty snippy in those days. After all, I'd been working by myself for a long time and was pretty independent.

"I don't know," he said. "I was waiting for Dotty."

"Turn us upside down," I said, "and we all look the same. Dotty's a nice girl but so am I. Come on upstairs."

I talked him into it and we made a two-person parade up the long winding staircase to my room. The way I looked at it, it was another five bucks for me. I didn't figure I was horning in on Dotty. She always had more work than she could handle anyway.

In my room the two of us got undressed and headed for the bed. I figured him for a straight trick but it didn't turn out to be that simple. He had a whole list of things he wanted me to do first, things I knew about and a few that were new to me. I didn't object. It was a living. Some of his notions turned my stomach a little but I didn't let on to him. I gave him his money's worth and he didn't seem to have any kick coming.

But Dotty wasn't happy.

She came into my room later that night and there was blood in her eye. "You little bitch," she yelled. "You come into this house and right away you think you got a right to horn in on my regulars. I ought to slap your face silly for a bit like that."

"You were busy," I reminded her. "And he didn't feel like waiting."

"He was a regular."

"So?"

"So he comes to me once a week and he tips me ten dollars every time he comes. So you stole him away from me, you little bitch."

Like I said, I was snotty in those days. And she was almost twenty years older than I was. I figured I could put her in her place.

"Look," I said, "maybe he used to be a regular of yours, old lady. He's not a regular any more. He found out what a young woman can do and he's not interested in an old biddie like you any more. So kindly get off my back or I'll kick your head in."

"Why, you—"

"Get out of here, Dotty. Or I'll push your ugly face in."

It was a stupid way for me to act. He was her trick and I should have let him wait for her. That's why I guess she figured she had to teach me a lesson. She taught me, all right.

She gave me a slap across the face. It hurt, but if I had a brain I would have taken it. I got mad and I swung right back at her. I hit her right in the breast and she gave a yell. And then we started.

She came for me with her nails flying. We tumbled onto the bed and she gave me the nails in the throat. They drew blood and I got madder than all hell. I hit her in the breast again right where I hit her the first time. This time I got her with my fist and it must have hurt because she tangled her hands in my hair and tried to pull it out by the roots.

I wanted to let out a yell but I knew better. All I had to do was wake up Mamie and she'd kick me out of that house so fast I wouldn't know what hit me. I kept my mouth shut, but Dotty went on yanking my hair and it hurt like hell.

I kicked her where it hurt and she let go. Then we went at it again. By now I was so mad I honest to God wanted to kill her. But she knew more about fighting than I did. Living in the Kitchen teaches you a lot about it, but so does hustling for twenty years. Dotty had me hands down.

She didn't play by the rules. She bit and she scratched and she kicked. By the time she left that room I was in such pain I could hardly move. My breasts were sore and I had huge black-and-blue marks on my arms and thighs. That was worse than the pain. In a high-class joint like Mamie's, a girl with bruises on her is a girl who's out of work for a few days.

I was mad at Dotty for a week. Then I cooled off, and it got so I could laugh about it. One thing was sure—I learned my lesson. I never made a play for one of her regulars after that. It was a good thing, because she probably would have killed me. She was like that.

There were things I liked about Mamie's house and things I didn't like at all. I stayed there a little more than a year, and looking back at it I can see that I had it pretty soft. If I had any brains I probably would have stayed put instead of leaving the way I did. But, as you may have figured out, I never had a monopoly on brains. And there were things about "housework," as we called it, that bothered me. I guess I was getting fussy.

Remember, the way I looked at it I was pretty hot stuff. I figured I ought to have the right to turn down a trick if I didn't like his looks or the way he acted. There were plenty of guys with pretty weird kicks who wanted me to do things I didn't want to do. A girl on her own can take her choice; a girl in a house gets what comes her way. Period.

On top of that, the five bucks out of each twenty kept looking smaller and smaller to me. That shows how dumb I was. I'm lucky if I can salt away half that much on a trick nowadays. But from where I sat, I was doing all the work while Mamie sat on her can and got all the money.

Another pain about "housework" was the routine. You tell the average person that hustling in a cathouse is routine and he'll laugh at you. But it's the truth. I worked a set number of hours whether I felt like it or not. During the day there was nothing to do except sit around my room or go to a movie.

I used to go to the movies with Honey all the time. She was the closest thing to a friend that I had in the house. We were together a lot, but all we could do was sit through a show or maybe go shopping. I did a lot of shopping in those days. Honey and I used to laugh about it. Here we were, spending all our money on dresses, and where could we wear them? Just to hustle in. That was all.

One afternoon was a panic. Honey and I were at the show, sitting through a couple of lousy mysteries, when two young guys hit on us and tried to pick us up. You know, make dates with us. I looked at Honey and she looked at me and I gave her a wink. What the hell!

We had until ten and that was plenty of time. We let the guys buy us a drink each and then we let them take us to the apartment where one of them was living. Honey and her guy went into the bedroom while I took my guy on the couch. It wasn't a money deal. They didn't know we were prostitutes. It was strictly for kicks.

And it was so good I couldn't believe it. Just having a party with a guy because you want to is wonderful, especially after you've been making a living at it for so long. My breasts tingled and my whole body came alive again. It was terrific.

"I needed that," Honey told me later. "A body gets lonely without a man. I really needed it."

"So did I."

She giggled. "They probably can't figure how come we were so anxious. Probably think they're supermen or something."

We laughed about it all the way back to Mamie's.

New York's Finest ...

You may have heard that there is no such thing as an honest cop. Don't believe it. There are honest cops. The thing is, they're all pounding beats in Canarsie. Or directing rush-hour traffic, maybe. One thing is sure. Very few of them are working for the Vice Squad.

The fix is a tough thing to explain. It exists on all levels of the rackets, from gambling to burglary. In prostitution it's the most important single element there is. Without it a whore cannot operate. With it she has hardly any worries.

The fix is why prostitution in this country is organized. It doesn't mean that you can't operate without belonging to the syndicate—except when it gets as greedy as it did in Lucky Luciano's day—but it does mean that when the heat is on, you may find yourself in trouble. It's a pretty complex setup and not many people understand it.

By spreading the right money to the right people, the syndicate makes sure that its people don't get arrested. The vice cops get paid, and the precinct captains get paid, and the big shots at central headquarters get their piece.

There are several different ways that the fix is placed. At

Mamie's house it was done on a straight percentage basis. A certain cut went to a syndicate operative who spread it around to keep the house clear. Other little bites went directly from Mamie to various cops who worked in our area, but the big bite went straight to the syndicate. That was headquarters for fixes.

If an individual pimp with a few girls in his stable wants to keep his girls out of jail, he has a similar arrangement with the syndicate. Instead of a percentage he can pay a flat rate depending on how many girls are working for him. A single girl hustling on her own works similarly, but it's tough for an independent hustler to make a connection. The mob prefers to get fix money in big hunks. They leave the independent hustlers to get arrested. After all, prostitution is illegal. Somebody has to take a fall now and then or the Vice Squad looks bad.

One hell of a boatload of money gets shelled out every week for protection. With all that dough floating around, it's impossible for a Vice Squad bull to stay honest. For one thing, his superiors don't want an honest man around. He just gets in their way, arresting the wrong people and making life tough for everybody. Besides, staying honest doesn't do him any good. If he arrests somebody and the fix is in, that somebody isn't going to stay arrested. The fix gets to the lieutenant, or to the judge, or to somebody somewhere along the line. The honest bull gets his face slapped and the girl goes free.

* * *

One Tuesday night after I'd been working at Mamie's place for a little over three months, I was sitting on my fanny waiting for something to happen when I heard voices in the front room.

"I hear you got a new one," a man was saying. "Figured I might as well come up and see how good she is."

Mamie said something I didn't catch. Then I heard the man again. He wasn't the whispering type. "Tell her she better be good," he said. "If she knows what's good for her."

Mamie came in, her face a little worried. She sat down next to me and started whispering. "The guy out there is a cop," she told me. "A detective on the Vice Squad. He's a miserable louse named Hanovan."

"So?"

"He's coming around for his own special brand of graft," she said. "You'd think a vice bull would have better things to do, wouldn't you? He ought to know enough about the business to quit getting his kicks this way. But not this bastard."

"He wants me?"

She nodded. "He tries out every new girl. It won't be a picnic but at least you'll get him out of the way. He never wants the same girl more than once. Hell, once is enough."

"What's so bad about him?"

"You'll see, Liz. But do whatever he tells you to do. He's rotten, but if he gets mad at you he could close this place in a minute. He's a powerful bastard. Just be nice to him and do anything he wants."

"Okay," I said. I tried not to look worried and she brought Hanovan in. It wasn't hard to see what he was—a sick, sick man—the kind that's got to be a louse in or out of uniform. He was a big lug with red hair and blue eyes and a tough way of walking. I hated him on sight. The way he looked at me made me feel dirty. His eyes were glazed and filled with hatred—his mouth curled in a sneer.

"What's your name?"

"Liz Crowley."

"I think I'll just call you whore, honey. That's enough of a name for you."

The bastard.

"Come on, whore. Get off your tail and let's see if you're good enough to stay in business."

I started upstairs and he followed me up. Halfway up the stairs I got a taste of what his private kick was. He reached out and pinched me, but it wasn't what you might call a friendly pinch. He pinched me as hard as he could and he pinched me in the most sensitive spot there is. It hurt like hell. I didn't have to turn around to know how glad he was that he had hurt me. It must have made him feel big. It takes a real big man to hurt a whore, believe me.

He kept his hands to himself until we got into my room and the door was shut. Then he grabbed me by the shoulders and hauled me up close to him. "You're the lowest thing there is. You're a disgrace to the human race. You're not fit to breathe the same air with the rest of the world."

I didn't say anything. I didn't know what in hell he wanted me to say so I kept my trap shut. Then he gave me a shove and I sailed halfway across the room and landed on my behind.

"Get up," he snapped, His voice was low, mean. "And get your goddamned clothes off. Fast!"

I started undressing. I was nervous and I had a little trouble with the buttons.

"Too slow," he growled. He came up to me and took hold of the front of my dress. It was a new one and it cost me twenty-five dollars. It was red, with a short skirt and lace at the collar. I liked it.

I guess he didn't like it. He ripped it right down the front, ripped it to ribbons.

"Now the rest."

I took off the rest of my clothes and stood there. He was fully dressed and I was stark naked and all he did was stare. Then he found something else to do.

"I'm going to punish you, whore. I'm going to slap you a little. You better not let out a sound. Not a sound, understand?"

I nodded. And then he got going. First, though, he had to swear at me and call me the filthiest names he could think of. Maybe it was to get his courage up. It takes a lot of guts to beat up a whore.

He slapped me across the breasts as hard as he could. I wanted to scream or fight back or something. But I knew better. I stood there and took it while he slapped one breast and then the other, forehand and then backhand, slapping them until they were practically raw. I can't even describe how painful it was. I don't want to think about it.

"Now something else," he said finally. "Get down on your knees, whore. Fast!"

I got down on my knees.

"Crawl!"

I crawled. He gave me a kick in the side and I was lucky I didn't get a broken rib out of the deal. He was wearing heavy shoes.

Then he took off his own clothes, everything but his shoes. "Crawl to me," he said. "Fast!"

I crawled to him.

"Now look up at me."

I looked up, wondering what was next, and he spat right in my face. "Don't wipe it off," he ordered. "There's more coming, whore."

There was. I had to stay where I was while he spat right in my face again and again. For some reason it was worse than the beating. It hurt deeper.

"Now," he said, "I want you to beg for it. Tell me how much you want me to do it to you. Beg me."

I begged, and he went on laughing at me and spitting. Then, finally, he grabbed me and heaved me on the bed. You could not call what we did "making love." There is only one word for it and it is unprintable. Finally he left and I sat on the edge of my bed and wished I could cry. I never felt so terrible in my life. But you know me. I couldn't cry a drop.

Mamie talked to me about him later. She told me I was lucky—most girls got it even worse than I did. "If he wasn't a cop he'd never get through the door," she told me. "Hell, if he was a square john with ideas like that I'd pay some heavies to beat the crap out of him. He's a real oddball, Liz—the meanest guy on the squad, but there's nothing I can do about him because he's got some kind of drag in the department."

I wished somebody would kill Hanovan. Finally, somebody did, just a few years ago. He "broke in" another hustler and made the mistake of going to sleep in her bed when he was finished. And the girl took good care of him.

She used a razor. She hated Hanovan with a passion, and there was one part of him she hated most of all. She used the razor on that part and he bled to death.

The poor little hustler didn't have a chance. Kill a cop and you get it in the neck. She got it in the neck, all right. They gave her life but she only lasted five years in prison. I heard she got pneumonia and died.

They should have given her a medal.

I had to take care of a few other cops while I worked at Mamie Donner's but none of them were like Hanovan. Even when they were relatively decent I couldn't stand them. With a regular trick, I was getting paid and I was giving the trick something in exchange. With a cop I was giving something for nothing. I had no choice. They made me feel more like a whore than when I was getting paid for it.

There's another sweet little fact about crooked cops that burns me, but good. You know, you hear stories about girls who became prostitutes and then want to quit but can't get out of it—how the madams and racketeers keep a girl in the business. Well, they're not so true now—not since Lucky Luciano had his wings clipped and had his tail tossed out of the country. It still happens, of course, but mostly it's the drug habit that makes a girl hustle, or her pimp, or she doesn't know what else to do. Sometimes, believe it or not, a perverted vice bull does the prodding.

Let me give you an example. I knew a girl—her name was Helen something-or-other—and she hustled for three years or so. Then she met a trick who turned out to be a hell of a nice guy and he wanted to marry her. This gave Helen a good out and she took it. She married the guy and things were fine for a while.

Then one day she was walking down the street and a fuzz made her from before. He knew she was a prostitute and he also knew she wasn't paying off. Hell, why should she pay off? She was out of the business.

This didn't mean anything to this bull. Helen had taken a fall once and all he had to do was testify against her and it was his word against hers. She knew she was licked. The bastard wanted a double payoff, money and flesh, and Helen had no choice. She gave him twenty dollars and let him go to bed with her.

It was pretty rotten. Here she was, a completely straight broad, and she had to take on this louse. Then she had to go back to her husband and pretend that everything was cool. It was bad enough the first time around, but it got worse when the cop developed a thing for Helen. He would hang around her neighborhood looking for her and every time he saw her it was another trip to the mattress. And all the while there wasn't a damned thing she could do about it. She had to take it and not say a word to anybody.

She tried staying home and that only made it worse. The rat came right into her own home and used the bed she shared with her husband. It was the filthiest thing in the world but that didn't make a bit of difference to the cop.

Helen didn't have a chance in hell. She loved her husband, really loved him, and it was only a matter of time before she went to him and told him all about it. He put in a complaint but got nowhere. Then the husband went to the cop and tried to beat the crap out of him. He weighed thirty pounds less and hadn't had a fight with anybody in years. The cop sent him to the hospital with his head in a sling.

Take it from there. The marriage went on the rocks and Helen went back in business. She found a pimp to put her in his stable and the cop found other broads to annoy. She had gone straight, remember, but she didn't have a chance. All because of that rat of a cop.

You can have most cops, as far as I'm concerned. They've made life miserable from the day they shot Mike Leary dead on the street. There are plenty of good ones, believe me, but prostitutes don't usually meet them.

I've often wondered why they don't make hustling legal and set up regular houses. That would solve the whole problem. What the hell—you don't clean up prostitution by passing a dumb law against it. That never does any good. If there are girls who want to hustle and men who want to sleep with them, all the laws in the world aren't going to do a bit of good.

But it won't ever be legal. Not with racket people making a fortune on it. Not with a lot of cops getting rich for looking the other way. Not in a million years.

Johnny the Pimp . . .

There were a lot of reasons for me to leave Mamie Donner's place of business—money, room to move, independence, things like that. But none of them were enough to get me out of there. I stayed for a year and I might have stayed for another five years if it hadn't been for Johnny. Johnny got me out of Mamie's house.

Johnny was a pimp.

He was ten years older than I was, twenty-nine to my nineteen, and he wasn't much for looks. He was a couple of inches taller than me, with shifty blue eyes and a weak chin. When he smiled he smiled just with his mouth instead of with his whole face, as if he didn't really mean to smile down deep inside. He had been a merchant seaman for a while and he had an anchor tattooed on his arm. But now he wasn't a sailor any more. Now he was a pimp.

You know what a pimp is? A pimp is a guy who lives with a prostitute and takes every penny she makes. A pimp spends her money on clothes for himself and a car for himself and a good time for himself, and if there's anything left he tells her to buy some food and cook for him. A pimp is the lowest thing in the world. A pimp is a rotten, lying rat, a sneaky swindler, a first-class, grade-A, number one son of a bitch.

Yet, a pimp is the only man in the world a whore can love.

It sounds silly but that's how it works out. You see, a hustler does a lot of pretty ugly things. One thing she isn't loaded to the teeth on is self-respect. She can't fall in love with a square john, one of her tricks, because she'll always feel like dirt compared to him. So when a whore is ready to fall in love, she picks a pimp. And she does this for a number of reasons.

First off, a pimp is lower than a prostitute is. I never had to put anything on with Johnny. He was John Gregg and I was Liz Crowley. He was a pimp and I was a hustler. We knew right where we stood and I never felt inferior to him.

And with Johnny I felt like a human being. With the tricks, I was always taking advantage of them. They were paying, and I was just lying there and performing like a trained seal, never feeling a goddamned thing. With Johnny I was doing the paying. It sort of balanced things out.

Mamie Donner didn't like the idea of her girls having pimps. But she knew better than to fight the whole routine. While I was working there, Sandy and Sally both had pimps, and so did two of the girls on the day shift. I thought they were nuts. Sandy once tried to explain it all to me and I still thought she was out of her skull. Imagine working like a Turk and then kicking in all of your dough to some weasel! It didn't make any sense to me.

Then I met Johnny. And I found out what it was all about.

We met on a movie date that Sandy arranged. All I knew

in advance was that there was this guy who knew what I was and wanted to take me out. I figured it would be a chance to relax, and it turned out to be even better than that. We had a great time.

He was a nice guy and a great talker. The way it seemed to me, all he wanted was to enjoy my company. And he didn't mind spending money. The date must have cost him better than fifty bucks, because after the movie we started hopping from one nightclub to another and he didn't seem to care what it cost him. Later I managed to dope out that it was an investment to him. He'd get it back in one night when I was hustling for him.

By the time that first date was over I was dying to sleep with him. I mean, here was a guy I didn't have to put on a front for and he liked me anyway. I was hoping he'd make a pass at me, but he played everything very cool. He just took me home. He didn't even kiss me.

I saw him again a week later and things were different. This time we went up to his apartment and he brought out a bottle of Scotch. He made big drinks and we sat there drinking them and listening to the radio.

"You're a sweet kid, Liz," he said. "I really go for you. You know that?"

I said something dumb, too mixed up to make much sense.

"You're very pretty," he went on. "And I like to be with you. You want to know something? I think I'm in love with you."

Was that a line? He sees me twice and suddenly he's in love with me. But nobody ever told me that before and I guess I wanted to hear it. Because right away I told him I was in love with him.

"Sit next to me, Liz. Over here on the couch."

I sat next to him and he took my chin in one hand and brought his lips down on mine. His mouth tasted of cigarettes and Scotch but I liked the taste this time. That first kiss did it for me. I wrapped my arms around him hard and pressed against him as tight as I possibly could. I hadn't felt like this since Mike Leary and that had been so long ago. Too long. I needed Johnny.

"My beautiful girl," he murmured. "My sweet, wonderful, beautiful girl. Let me undress you, Liz."

I was wearing a skirt and sweater and he took them off of me. Then I was in my bra and panties and he wasn't touching me at all, just looking at me and telling me what a beautiful body I had. He reached for me and his hands on my shoulders made me start shaking inside. Then he unhooked my bra and took it off, his eyes riveted to my breasts.

"They're lovely," he said. He started stroking them, his hands skillful on them, and the world started going around for me. My skin tingled and my heart was beating like all the clocks in the world. He made me lie down on the couch and crouched over me, kissing my breasts and fondling them until I couldn't take it any more. I had to have him or I would go out of my mind.

We didn't even go to the bedroom. We just stayed on that couch and made the world take a swim for itself. What we did wasn't very complicated or anything. It was just love, straight and simple, and it was the nicest and sweetest thing that had ever happened to me.

When it was over I held him in my arms and looked up into his blue eyes. It was raining outside and I listened to the rain and thought about Johnny. I would do anything he ever wanted me to do. Anything at all. If he told me to cut off one of my fingers I'd ask him which one. He was my man and I needed him and that was all there was to it.

From that point on everything went according to plan. I left Mamie's the next day. After all, Johnny and I were in love, weren't we? So, natch, I ought to be living with him. But the fact that we were in love had nothing to do with the way I earned my living. I was a hustler and I went right on hustling. It didn't even seem wrong to me.

"Just for a little while," Johnny said. "I've got big plans, Liz. You'll see, baby. We'll get some money saved and I'll buy a club. There's a spot I've got my eye on, baby. A little nightclub down in the Village that can be a gold mine with the right management. Once we get enough money saved, we'll buy that club and live on Easy Street. And you deserve it, baby. Nothing's too good for my girl."

Corny? Sure it was. But I swallowed it. I wanted to believe it, and when you want to believe something you can swallow any line in the world. We needed money to buy the club, so I went out and hustled and turned as many tricks as I could. Johnny didn't do a damned thing. The way he put it, I could make a hell of a lot more money than he could, so there wasn't much point in his working at all.

And that's the way it went. We lived in a nice little pad on 70th Street near Columbus. At night I would go out and hustle. I wasn't on Eighth Avenue then—I was better material than streetwalker stuff, at the time. I hustled at three little bars on Lex in the mid-Fifties, letting guys pick me up to take me back to the apartment. My price was anywhere from twenty to forty, depending on how much I could talk the trick into paying. I made as much as three hundred dollars a day or as little as a hundred. Whatever I made, every cent went to Johnny for the nightclub. Of course, there wasn't any nightclub. He spent every cent of it on himself. I must have realized even then where the money was going. He wore hundred-dollar suits and ten-dollar shirts and forty-dollar shoes. He picked up a car—a powder-blue Caddy convertible. That's where my money went, but I pretended not to realize it. Just like you can make yourself believe a lie if you want to believe it, you can ignore the truth if it's too much for you. At least I could.

It was a rotten deal for me and I loved every minute of it. For the first time in years I felt alive. Johnny was my man and I was his woman. That made up for a lot of things.

We didn't go out night-clubbing and he didn't spend money on me, but there were more important things. I had a man to talk to, a man to be with, a man who could make me happy in the hay. I was only half a whore now, the way I saw it. When Johnny and I were alone I was a woman and he was a man. We were perfectly respectable people in our own little world.

So the months passed and I went on turning tricks. I managed to build up a list of regulars—guys who came to see me two or three times a month. I made good money and Johnny kept telling me he loved me. It could have been worse.

"Liz? Come here, baby. I got something for you."

He was in the bedroom. I put the groceries in the kitchen and went in to him. He was on the bed with a bunch of small brown cigarettes in one hand. The ends were twisted and the cigarettes were very thin. I wasn't square. I was a racket broad and I knew what he was holding. Marijuana.

"Pot," he said. "You ever make pot?"

"No."

"We're gonna make it, baby. We are going to walk very tall and fly very high and see many extraordinary things. Sit by me."

"Isn't it habit forming?"

He laughed. "Not pot," he said. "Hard stuff is. Pot is just a kick. Let's cook, baby."

He put one of the joints between his lips and lit it with the gold lighter he had bought for himself. He didn't smoke it the way you smoke a regular cigarette. He held it between his thumb and forefinger and drew the smoke straight into his lungs in very long drags, keeping his lips slightly parted so that he took in air along with the smoke. He showed me how to do it and I tried it. It burned my throat a little and didn't taste very good. The first few times I coughed and he bawled me out for wasting the smoke. Then I caught on and we smoked all the sticks.

I looked at Johnny. His eyes were slightly glazed and he kept them half-open. He looked very cool, completely relaxed.

"You there, baby?"

At first I didn't feel anything. Then I managed to relax and I found out what it was all about. I felt wonderful, my arms and legs all light and airy, my mind very keen and clear. I learned later that marijuana doesn't actually clear your mind. You just *think* it does. But that's enough. If you think it's clear, it is.

I guess what pot does is make everything a little more intense. When Johnny touched me I felt it all through me. I wanted him right away and he wanted me. We got undressed and made love and it was very good. I can't describe it too well. It was just that I could feel everything completely, everything that was happening. It seemed to last forever and when we were done I fell asleep at once.

That was the first time I ever smoked pot. I was nineteen then. The most recent occasion I ever had it was about a week ago. I've smoked it off and on ever since Johnny turned me on to it for the first time. He was telling the truth for once—in a way. It isn't habit-forming, but it can send you on to the hard stuff—addictive drugs like heroin and morphine and cocaine.

It did with Johnny.

It took him three months. Then one day he came home to me, not with a handful of little brown cigarettes but with a surprise. The surprise consisted of a junkie's kit—a hypodermic needle, a spoon, a match, a capsule of heroin.

"Just a little skin-popping," he told me. "Just a quick shot for a booster. No mainline action." By this he meant that he would only take a shot in the fleshy part of his arm instead of shooting the heroin directly into a vein. There's a theory that you can't get hooked this way. You'd better not believe it.

I watched him while he cooked the heroin on a spoon and filled the needle with it. Then he put the needle in his arm and gave himself a shot. It didn't take long to hit. His eyes got completely glassy and he went on the nod. That means he took a nap right away.

I didn't want to take a shot but he talked me into it. I was damned lucky. I took that one shot and I never took another one. I knew a few girls like this. Some people, the lucky ones, can stop after their first shot and stay away from the stuff forever. But I never met anybody who took more than one shot without winding up an addict. There probably are people who managed it, but I never met one.

As I said, I was lucky. My first shot was also my last shot. That's not how it worked out with Johnny. According to him, he wasn't going to get hooked. Not my Johnny. He was too smart to get himself hooked. He knew how to keep clear.

Sure he did.

First it was a skin-pop a day. Then it was two a day. Then it was a mainline shot. "What the hell, Liz. No sense wasting it when you can mainline it. You get a bigger kick that way. Might as well get your money's worth, huh? Right, baby?"

Right as rain. In no time at all my man was a junkie, an addict, a guy who would crawl up the walls if he didn't get his needle on time. It was a shot every few hours by then. He was high all the time, except by now junk didn't really give him much of a high. It kept him alive. He had to have a shot every few hours in order to feel the least bit human.

I had to hustle like nobody had to hustle before. Heroin costs money, big money. Johnny had a fifty-dollar-a-day habit in no time at all. $350 a week is a lot of money to spend on junk. That's why it's impossible for a junkie to keep out of the rackets. Even with a habit half the size of Johnny's, that's still almost two bills a week for white powder. And the only way a junkie can haul down that kind of bread is in the rackets. He's in no condition to hold a steady job—and certainly not one that pays that kind of money.

To make things just that much groovier, Johnny was in no condition to be much of a bedmate. When you're a junkie you don't have any interest in horizontal parlor games. So now he was getting all my money and I wasn't getting a thing. And do you want to know something? *I loved the son of a bitch more than ever.*

Because he needed me now. He needed me a hundred percent and I *wanted* to be needed. I loved him so hard it wasn't funny. I would have died for him. I didn't have to. It went the other way around.

I must have a magic touch or something. I'm the original kiss of death. There was Mike Leary and there was Mom and there was Johnny. Whenever I love somebody they're as good as dead. But with Johnny it was a little different. I was real lucky. I got to watch him die.

We were in the bedroom and he was taking a shot. I was helping him, cooking up the heroin for him because his hands were shaking. I gave him the needle and he put it into his arm. I don't know how he found a spot for it. He was all needle marks by then.

He looked at me and his eyes were wide. I could see he was in pain. He grabbed hold of his chest and he went white.

"Liz—"

He opened his mouth wide, pitched over on his face and didn't move. And that was that. He was dead as a lox. It was a standard way for a junkie to go—an overdose. That's a big danger in junk. You never know how much you're taking, and if it's too much, you're dead. And Johnny was dead.

I sat with him for three hours, wanting to cry but not making it. Then I got out of there, walked around the block, came home again and called the fuzz. They examined me, found out I wasn't a junkie and let me go. They had no reason to hold me. As far as they were concerned, he was just another dead junkie.

I have never felt so completely alone in my life. That night I sat around feeling lousy. But the next day I really went to work. All of a sudden I needed money, and I earned as much as I could, as fast as I could.

Johnny had the best funeral human flesh could buy.

You Meet the Strangest People...

After you hustle for a few years you begin to think that half the men in the world are weirdos. You know, perverts. That's because a guy with a twisted kind of a kick has to go to a prostitute if he wants to get his jollies. Even if he's married, his wife would get sick if he asked her to do certain things for him. And he wouldn't dream of asking. Hell, a guy wouldn't expect his own wife to do something filthy. For that sort of scene he'd go to a professional—a girl who wouldn't have any choice in the matter.

You really meet all kinds of oddballs in this business. At first it used to get me sick—not just what I was doing, but the type of sick, messed-up men who were coming to me. You wouldn't believe some of the things they wanted me to do to them. Look—just imagine the strangest and nuttiest thing you can think of, something that no guy could possibly get any kick out of. It's an odds-on bet that some cat gets his kicks that way. No matter how crazy it sounds, somewhere in this world there's a guy who loves it.

Let me get one thing straight. By weirdos I don't mean guys who happen to want a little variety in their sex. Most tricks are like that to a degree. A trick will come to me, for example, and have some brand-new position that he thinks he managed to dream up all by himself. This to me is normal. And the same thing goes for guys who prefer French and Greek variations in their love play. A girl who isn't ready to go along with these crazy requests just isn't going to make much money. It's part of the business.

No, when I talk about weirdos I mean the real first-class nuts. For example, there are jerks who would pay a hustler to let them beat her up. I always stayed away from this sort of scene. Some guys lose control and you wind up in the hospital. I dodged that type of nut, except for that cop Hanovan when I had no choice. But when a hustler gets older she has to take whatever she can get. If a guy wants to beat her up she takes it. Maybe that's what'll happen to me in a few years, when I'm too old to make good money any other way. God, I hope not. I hate getting hurt. I don't know if I can take it.

Other tricks like it the other way around. They lay out big dough to get beaten. I remember one guy who came around just a week or two ago with a cane. He didn't even want me to take off my clothes. He took off his clothes and stretched out on the bed on his stomach and told me to give it to him across the behind. I whaled the tar out of him for a few minutes and then he was happy. The way I look at it, a guy has to be pretty sick to get his kicks out of being hurt.

Weirdos, weirdos, weirdos. Did you happen to know that there are certain guys who get a special kick out of making it with a pregnant woman? The more pregnant she is, the bigger their kick. Other guys want you to pretend they're raping you. You have to struggle and scream and kick or it's no fun for them.

Weirdos. You know, some girls try to figure out what it is that makes a weirdo get the kicks he gets. Not me. I don't really care what it is. The way I look at it, they're paying and I'm taking care of them. Period. Once they're gone I try to forget about them. They give me a funny feeling in my stomach, like it's too empty.

Maybe they might interest you. If you want to figure them out, go right ahead. It's your business. I'll just tell you about a few of them.

About a month after Johnny took his overdose, I was hustling over at the Royal Arms on Lexington and 52nd Street. The bar was a mob joint and the fix was in solid. I had to pay plenty to hustle there but I had no worries about getting busted. I was sitting at the bar in a very low-cut dress with a good part of me hanging out of it. I had my legs crossed and I was wearing a dress that only reached my knees to begin with, so most of my legs were showing. A guy hit on me and I guess he liked what he saw. There was a lot to see. At any rate, he came over and asked if he could buy me a drink.

I looked him up and down. He was tall and well built, a pretty good-looking guy around thirty or so. I should have figured right off the bat that he was a pervert. A guy with looks like that doesn't have any trouble getting it for free if he wants straight stuff. I wasn't thinking good that night.

"Forget the drink," I told him. "You don't just want to drink, do you? Why waste your money on liquor?"

He smiled. "You're a bright girl," he said.

"A good one, too."

"Then let's get out of here."

We waltzed out of the place arm in arm, and outside he told me what he wanted. He wasn't ashamed to talk about it the way so many of the perverted ones are. He came right out and said it.

"I want you to come up to my place," he said. He had a very cultured way of speaking, enunciating his words clearly and carefully. I told him I'd just as soon go to his place and he smiled.

"What I want to do," he said, "is quite simple. There is another man at my apartment, just a boy, actually. I want you to let him make love to you. While the two of you make love, I will watch."

"That's all?"

"That's all."

That was okay with me. The guy didn't look like the watchbird type but you never know. Lots of guys get their kicks that way. Some of them like to look at a man and a prostitute together, and others want to watch two girls. I looked him over and decided he was rich enough to pay heavy. I asked for fifty dollars and he didn't even try to talk me down.

We took a cab to his pad, which turned out to be in

Greenwich Village. He lived on the top floor of a new brick building and the pad was really something to look at. A thick carpet, paintings on the walls, plush furniture. You get the idea.

Then he introduced me to the kid I was supposed to make it with. He was even better looking than my trick and much younger, no more than eighteen, tops. He had curly blond hair and a slim, neat figure. I figured I could have done a lot worse.

"This is Adam," my trick said. "And the bedroom is right through that doorway."

We went right through the doorway and there was the bedroom. The bed was a big one and I was impressed. We were going to do this in style. We didn't waste any time. My trick plopped himself down in a chair and Adam and I got our clothes off. He was built very well.

It always gives me a funny feeling to work with somebody watching. Adam played things nice and slow, giving me a real working over before we got down to business. He fondled me and kissed me as if he knew what it was all about. Believe it or not, I was really beginning to get all worked up. I ran my hands over his back and his skin was soft as silk. I couldn't keep my hands off of him, especially the way he was getting me so excited.

When we got down to brass tacks I really let myself go. I even got so I forgot my trick was watching. Maybe it was because Adam wasn't the one who was paying the fare. That way I didn't feel the contempt for him that a hustler always feels for a trick. I had a chance to relax and enjoy it. And did I enjoy it!

It was the best in a long time and when it was finally over I was so limp I couldn't move. I wanted to lie there forever.

Then my trick was saying: "Now it's my turn."

That bugged me. I mean, fifty bucks is a nice price, but I thought I was only going to have to take on one of them. And after a round with Adam I wasn't in shape to have another go at it. I was all set to bitch about it a little but I didn't have a chance.

Because I found out what my trick was talking about. It was his turn, all right. But not with me. No, sir.

With Adam.

I absolutely couldn't believe it. I stood there like a dumbbell while my trick and Adam did a few things that I'd just as soon not think about any more. You want to figure out weirdos? Figure that one out, why don't you? And if you can make any sense of it, clue me in. It beats the hell out of me. Or better yet, *don't* clue me in. I'd just as soon forget the whole thing.

If you think he was one for the books—and if you don't, brother, then there must be something wrong with *you*—then you ought to hear about another sweetheart. This trick I sort of liked, actually. He came around about a dozen times, once a month for a year or so, and every time we went through the same routine. He was sort of fun, and every time he came around I made the easiest twenty-five there could possibly be. But if you want to talk about oddballs, this boy took the cake.

The first time I saw him, he wasn't a trick. Not exactly. He encountered me on the street, a dumpy little guy carrying a rolled umbrella, and he asked if he could talk to me. I had nothing better to do. So we talked, and it turned out he wanted to make an appointment. He had a special bit he wanted me to go through, and he wanted it set up so that when he got to my place we could go right into the bit without having to talk about it first. He talked and I listened. It sounded nutty to me, but I wasn't going to complain about it. Money is money, and this was going to be a cinch and a half.

I never figured he would show. I thought maybe his kick was just talking to hustlers and then standing them up, but I waited for him and he got there right on time. I went into the bit right off the bat.

"Darling," I said. "I've been waiting for you for so long! Oh, my darling. My sweet, my love. I need you so much!"

He came inside and sat down in a soft chair while I played it from beginning to end. I took off my clothes while he watched me. I took off every last stitch and kept telling him how much I wanted him. Then I knelt in front of him on the floor and looked up at him, begging him to make love to me. And all this time he was sitting there with a sort of pleased expression on his face, just taking it all in and not saying a word.

"Do anything you want with me," I begged. "Anything in the world. Kick me, beat me, pound my breasts until they ache. Love me any way you want to."

He sat there like a bump on a log and smiled like an idiot.

Then I started telling him what I wanted to do to him, how

I wanted to caress him, things like that. I begged and pleaded, and the dope just sat there taking it all in.

Then he stood up. "No," he said. "I'm sorry, but I don't want to have anything to do with you. I'm leaving."

And away he went, happy as could be, grinning from ear to ear.

Every month for a year we played that scene, and every damned time there would be an envelope with twenty-five bucks in it waiting for me. That was his kick. He wanted me to beg him to love me, and then he would refuse, and that would be that. I didn't have to do a thing in the world. I was naked, of course, but that was just part of the act. He hardly even looked at my body. He just kept his dumb eyes on my face and listened to me beg for it. It was the strangest bit I ever went through in my life.

You know, the funny part is he began to get to me. I started wondering why he was so special he could turn me down like that, and I had to remind myself that it was only an act and I wanted him about as much as I wanted a dose of v.d. Can you imagine a guy with a kick like that? He didn't want to *do* anything. He didn't want to *see* anything. He just wanted to be asked, and then to have the great thrill of turning me down.

The world is full of them, one nuttier than the next. Anything you can think of, there's some dope who's all hot to go for it. There were a couple guys who paid me to read pornography aloud to them, and another lunatic who paid me to listen while he read pornography to *me*. There was a jerk who just wanted to kiss my feet for half an hour, and, sure enough, another moron who paid me to kiss *his* feet. The world is full of morons.

I used to hate them. I'm not kidding. I really hated them. I hated their guts. But lately I don't mind them so much any more. They have their kick and they don't bother anybody. What the hell, it takes all kinds to make the world the way it is. I'm not going to fight about it. It's their business.

But one thing I'll never do is get used to them. I've gotten used to being a doormat and I've gotten used to ducking cops. I've gotten used to hating myself in the morning, to thinking about cutting my throat, to feeling so rotten inside I can't stand it another minute.

But I haven't gotten used to the weirdos. They're just a little too far out for me.

Some Girls Who Weren't . . .

I mentioned Kim before. Maybe you remember her. She worked at Mamie's house and she was built like a boy with very small breasts and slender hips. Her hair was short and black. As I think I mentioned, she was a lesbian.

I suppose that sounds kind of nutty. I mean, you would think that the last business in the world for a gay girl to get into would be hustling. You would be wrong. I've known dozens of lesbian prostitutes in the years that I've been in the business. They make money with men and make love with each other. I knew a call girl once, a classy blonde with the world's biggest breasts. She got fifty to a hundred a night. And the only way she could get any fun out of sex was with another woman. Now, you'll have to agree with me, that's real nutty.

I knew a madam who made her girls sleep with her or work somewhere else. I never worked for her, but I knew one girl who did and she said the whole scene was quite an experience. Every last girl in the house was as gay as a jay. When the customers went home for the evening, that was when things really got going. The girls would get together in the parlor and choose up sides for the evening. Once they were paired off they headed for their rooms and really went to work. If the customers could have seen them they would have flipped.

It may sound silly, but it makes more sense than you might think at first. To understand it, you've got to see how a lot of hustlers feel about men. That's simple enough—they hate them. You take the average hustler and the picture comes out like this—a man seduced her in the first place, another man got her started hustling, other men, cops, arrest her and make her pay off, and more men are her customers, having her day in and day out and not showing her a thing.

When a girl lives a life like this, pretty soon she can't get a thing out of a relationship with a man. Every man to her is a trick, a sucker, a louse, a rat. And yet, let's face it, the girl needs sex—she needs tenderness.

So a lot of these man-hating girls become lesbians. It fits in a hundred percent. That way they have what you might call a sexual outlet without having anything to do with a man. It keeps their love life apart from their business, if you follow me. Besides, that way they can feel better when they're with tricks. A gay hustler will think to herself, *This grunting and straining pig isn't showing me a thing. I'm cheating him, I'm faking him out, because I'm a lesbian and he's not doing anything to me.*

I was never quite like that. Men are rotten, most of them, like that bastard Riordan who raped me and that cop Hanovan who made my life miserable. But I've met a few decent guys. Some men are good and some stink. I don't hate all of them. Just the rotten ones.

But even so I've had what they call homosexual experiences. It's a different sort of scene with me because the gay kick was never a very big part of my life. But I've done it more than once and I've gotten a great deal of pleasure out of it. I won't deny it.

Look at it this way. Since I turned pro thirteen years ago, there has never been a month in my life, except the time when I was in jail, when I did not make love to a hundred men. Usually it was at least triple that. I've done everything there is to do. How much kick can be left in it?

So doing it with a girl can bring a little variety into the act. If I get a thing going with another hustler, we are equals. Neither of us is paying the other and neither of us is taking advantage of the other. It's just a change of scene.

Gee, maybe you'll be thinking I'm as nuts as the weirdos I was talking about a chapter back. That's not the way I see it at all. From where I sit, things look different. I sell love every single damned day. I figure I'm entitled to anything I can get on my own.

But let me tell you about Kim. That was the first time, and it was pretty interesting. Kim was a good kid. I always liked her.

It was a dog of a day at Mamie's. I couldn't sleep any more and there was nothing better to do. My friend Honey was out with a guy and I was sitting on my hands and waiting for night to come. That room of mine was beginning to feel like a prison. I couldn't take it much longer—just sitting on my bed like a dope and staring at the four walls.

There was a knock on the door and I yelled *Come in* without waiting to find out who it was. I didn't care. Anybody was better than being alone. The door opened and it was Kim.

"Hi, Liz. You busy? I just thought I'd drop in for a minute."

"I'm glad you did," I told her. "I'm going batty in here."

"Bored, huh?"

"You said it. This place is getting on my nerves."

"I know what you mean," she said. She sat down on the bed next to me and it made me feel naked. She was wearing a blouse and skirt and all I had on was a thin wrapper. What the hell, I thought. It didn't matter. We were both girls. Still, it made me feel a little bit funny. It was the way she was looking at me, staring at my breasts.

"You sure have a nice shape," she said. "Especially in the chest department. Looking at you makes me feel like a man."

That had a double meaning that sailed on past me. "You're a good-looking girl," I said. "You don't have to be jealous of these things."

"Not jealous," she said. "Just admiring."

I said something about how dull it was just sitting around the house and she agreed. "You must get lonesome," she said. "You must wish there was someone for you to relax with. I know I feel that way a lot of the time."

"That's how I feel."

"You can relax with me, Liz."

I thought it was a funny thing for her to say. I should have been able to put it all together—the looks, the talk, the friendship bit. But I was new to the business. Kim was the first lesbian I had ever met, and at the time I had no idea she was gay. The idea never even entered my mind.

We talked, and I relaxed, and all of a sudden it started. We were just sitting there and before I knew what was happening she was kissing me. It caught me completely by surprise. Her lips touched mine and her arms went around me. It was the first time any girl ever did anything like that to me.

Then, all at once, she let go. We sat there looking at each other and I didn't know what to make of it. I felt ashamed for some reason and I didn't know what in hell I was ashamed of.

"You don't get it, do you?"

I stared at her.

"Listen to me, Liz. You poor kid, you really don't know what's coming off, do you? Liz, there are things women can do together. Nice things. Much better than the things a woman does with a man. Two women together can make the sweetest love in the world. Sweeter than sugar. It's good and it's sweet and it's clean."

"But—" I stopped there. I was seeing her differently now. She was still Kim, but she didn't seem like a friend. She was more like a lover and I didn't know what to say or what to think. I was lost.

"I want to make love to you, Liz. I'll make you feel better than you ever felt in your life. Let me touch you, Liz. Let me touch you and kiss you. You don't have to do a thing. Just let me love you."

I wasn't excited but I wasn't disgusted, either. When you hustle for a living it takes a lot to disgust you. I didn't push her away when she reached for me this time. I wanted to see what would happen.

At first it was funny, having Kim kiss me. Then the kisses changed from pecks on the mouth to serious stuff, with her tongue probing deeply into my mouth and her arms strong around me. I didn't resist when she pushed me back down on the bed and took my wrapper off. Her eyes were shining when she looked at my breasts and her hands were soft as feathers when she began to touch them.

"They're beautiful, Liz. Now I'm going to kiss them and fondle them and I'm going to drive you out of your mind. You'll go wild, little Liz."

She was right. She knew what to do, knew it better than any man I had ever been with. Her lips and hands were clever and adept and pretty soon I was as hot as a two-dollar pistol.

"Take off your clothes, Kim. I want you naked, too."

She withdrew from me then and my breasts itched, wanting her to touch them again. Then she was taking off her clothes and she was naked with me. She took me in her arms and I ran my hands all over her body. Her skin was much softer than any man's. I loved to touch her.

Then she let me kiss her breasts. They were much smaller than mine but they were firm and neatly shaped. I felt kind of funny. I never did anything like that before. But I didn't mind, and Kim sure as hell enjoyed it.

Then, suddenly, we were lying close together, flesh to flesh, our mouths hotly joined and in a little while I found myself lost in a violent, dizzying whirl of sensation while Kim kept moaning and whispering endearments to me.

Kim and I never had what you would call an affair. We made love two or three times after that and it was pretty good every time, although not as nice as it was with Johnny Gregg. I met him not long after that, and that was when I moved out of the house. That ended everything with Kim, of course. I never saw her again.

Naturally, I didn't make love with another girl while I was living with Johnny. There were a couple of times when another girl and I would put on a show for two men, and then each of the men would take one of us. But that was strictly for show. Watching us perform would get the men all excited. For us it was just part of the act, the same as when we did it with the men.

I had a few brief flings with girls after Johnny died. It was because I was very lonely, and I didn't want to get tied up with another pimp.

One time I was hustling at a bar on Lex and I decided to call it quits for the night. I got to talking with Shirley Simmons, a pretty little blonde a year or two younger than myself.

She was lonely, too, and pretty depressed. We had a few drinks together and went up to my place. One thing led to another and we wound up in bed.

It was the first time Shirley ever did anything like that and I guess I was a little like Kim. I know I got excited when I kissed and fondled Shirley's breasts. She was shorter than I was, but her breasts were about twice the size of mine. I didn't think another girl's breasts could excite me but Shirley's did.

Our affair was different from the one Kim and I had. Kim was sort of a masculine type, but Shirley and I were both definitely feminine. It was a real equal sort of thing. It was a welcome change for both of us, and it ended the horrible loneliness that is the worst single thing about being a prostitute. Shirley moved in with me and we both hustled there and kicked in for the rent. We slept together only when we happened to feel like it and neither of us had any claim on the other. Once in a while we would put on shows if a couple of tricks happened to want us to.

It ended when Shirley got busted for disorderly conduct. She drew sixty days and promised to come and see me when she got out of the tank. But I never saw her again and I never received any word about her. I wonder how she made out. I hope everything broke right for her. She was a good kid and the two of us were pretty close.

*　　　*　　　*

There's another connection between lesbianism and prostitution that not many people know about. It doesn't happen very often, for some reason, but it comes up now and then. I'm talking about a lesbian who pays a prostitute to go to bed with her.

As I said, it doesn't happen very often. Most lesbians prefer to stick to their own. But I've heard stories, and I've even been there once or twice.

It never happened in Mamie's and it never happened when I was living with Johnny. It didn't happen until recently, when I wasn't good enough for "housework" or Lexington Avenue bars any more. I was on Seventh Avenue holding up a building and waiting for something to happen when the woman came over to me.

At first I thought she was another hustler. She could have been—that's the only kind of woman you see on the block where I was working. But this one was too well-dressed for Seventh Avenue, and too old for Lexington. She was about thirty-five and she was wearing a fur jacket and shoes with very high heels.

Her voice was husky. "Walk along with me," she said. It took me a second at the most before I got the message. I walked along with her and she made the pitch.

"I want us to go to your room," she told me. "And I want us to make love together. Is that all right with you?"

All right with me? I'm Liz Crowley, the anything-for-a-buck kid. Friend, anything in the world is all right with me.

The fur jacket meant money and the fact that she was a

lesbian meant that I could probably get a better price than I would have gotten from a man. I'm ten-dollar merchandise nowadays, but I told this dame the price was thirty. She didn't haggle. I took her to my cruddy room on 47th Street and she told me what I was supposed to do.

Fun it wasn't. The gal was Miss Passive of 1902. She wanted me to do all the work, and some of the things she wanted me to do were not very nice. To top it off, she had a pretty rotten body. It's funny—with a male trick I never care what he looks like. But this trick was a woman and I'd never had a woman trick before. Somehow the fact that she was a mess put me off a little.

But thirty dollars is thirty dollars. Little Liz did what she was expected to, and Miss Frigid Bitch had no complaints coming when all was said and done. She got her money's worth, damn her.

When the ball game was over she was cool as a cucumber with goose pimples. She got dressed very quickly and then went over to the mirror to make up her face. That gave me the shakes. I never took care of a trick and then watched her put on lipstick. It was quite an experience, believe me.

"That was very nice, my dear," she said. "I had a lovely time."

I didn't say anything.

Then the stupid broad started laughing. I couldn't figure out what was supposed to be such a riot, but there wasn't much I could do to shut her up. So I let her laugh.

"I was just thinking," she said. "If he could only have seen me a few minutes ago."

"Who?"

"My husband," she said. "My poor, dumb, trusting husband."

That picked me up and threw me on my tail. The bitch had a husband yet. Suddenly I was feeling sorry for the poor sap. To be married to a woman like that—that was one for the books.

I looked at the broad and got mad. I didn't care if I didn't get her business again—business like that I can live without.

"Don't worry about your husband," I snapped. "With a wife like you he's probably a customer of mine."

And you know, it didn't faze her. She gave me a sickening grin and reached over to pat me on the behind. "I wouldn't mind," she said. "You've got enough for both of us, dear. Maybe we'll come up and see you together."

And then, thank God, she was gone. I took a long, hot shower afterward, but I felt dirty anyway.

STRAIGHT AND NARROW ...

I was seventeen when I started selling myself and twenty-four when I quit.

No, don't go back and read the last paragraph over. You got it right the first time around. I quit hustling six years ago. Did you ever quit smoking? Are you smoking now? Yeah, that's how I quit hustling. I got a feeling that the only thing anybody ever quits for good is living.

I quit hustling because I met a guy and we sort of fell in love with each other. It comes out corny when I think about it but you can believe me when I say there wasn't anything corny about it. It was a damned good part of my life. Sometimes it hurts to remember it because of the way it ended, but I remember it anyway because there was something awfully good about the whole thing.

It wasn't like the movies or the confession stories. The guy I fell in love with wasn't a nice, respectable, square John from Murray Hill. Nothing like that ever works out. There's a gulf between racket girls and square tricks that all the decency in the world can't bridge. And he wasn't a noble schmuck saving me from a life of sin, either. If there was any saving going on, we were both doing it. Or trying to.

His name was Phil Notaro and he was a punk. He wrote numbers and pulled an occasional holdup. Once in a while he stole a car. A real big shot. He grew up on 37th Street, just a couple of blocks from where I grew up. That was something we both got a bang out of.

He wasn't tall, dark and handsome. He was short, dark and ugly and I loved him and he loved me. He was a punk and I was a whore and we fell in love, and if you think that's just too funny for words you can go and drop dead for yourself.

It didn't start romantic. We met in a movie on 42nd Street in the middle of the afternoon. Where else can a hustler go at that time of day? Drop into a 42nd Street movie in the afternoon and half the girls you see there are racket broads. Anyway, I was there in the balcony, and so was he, and we got to talking. God knows what we talked about. When the show ended we walked out together. I thought maybe he was a trick but he didn't come on like a trick. He was too hip.

"Let's get some coffee, Liz."

"Well—"

"Come on. We'll pretend we're a couple of squares on a date. I can use coffee."

His nose was crooked and he was missing a pair of teeth in front. But he combed his hair neatly and bathed regularly. His clothes were cheap but well chosen and he wore them well. He had thick, dark eyebrows and honest eyes.

We had coffee and toasted English at Bickford's and then for some reason we went to my place and to bed. I don't know why. The love-at-first-sight bit is something I never did believe in. Call it sex if you want. A hustler has a right to need a man just like anybody else does. So we went to bed, and Phil was different from any man I had ever been with before. There was an honesty in his lovemaking that got through to me. He wasn't like a trick and he wasn't like Johnny. He was honest, and it was good for me and good for him.

He sat on the edge of the bed afterwards and started getting dressed again. "What hours do you hustle, Liz?"

"Nine to five—bankers' hours."

He laughed. "Then you go to sleep?"

"Usually."

"And wake up when?"

"Noon or abouts. Why?"

He shrugged. "I thought I might drop over every once in a while. If you didn't mind. Today was pretty good, Liz. And I could tell it was good for you."

"It was."

"If I come by around noon some day would I be welcome? Just to sit around is good enough. I don't want you to think I'm just trying to get something for free."

"I know better."

"Well, I—"

I felt funny. "Phil," I suggested, "why don't you just move in?"

"I couldn't do that."

"It would save on the rent—"

He laughed again. "I'm not a pimp, Liz. I don't live off anybody but myself, least of all a woman."

"You could pay your share—"

He held up a hand. "Sure, I could," he said. "Liz, I know a little about the game. I know how much dough a hustler can bring in and I also know how much dough I make. Big money sometimes, but lately things haven't been moving too well. Inside of a week you'd be paying for everything. In another week I'd be taking money from you. That's not my kind of scene."

We let it lie. He was right, I guess. And I didn't want to support a pimp. Some girls float from one pimp to the next but once was enough for Liz Crowley. We sat around for a few more minutes. Then he left and I got ready to go talk some suckers into sleeping with me.

He dropped over a few days later and, as it happened, we didn't make love. It happened to be the wrong time of the month for that sort of thing. This was a shame in one sense but good in another. That meant the evening was free. We were together for about fifteen hours, having a couple of drinks together, getting a bite at a restaurant around the corner, talking our heads off hour after hour. I hadn't talked to anybody in a long time—I mean really talking where you don't have your guard up all the time. I enjoyed it. It was more fun than sex.

I didn't see him for three days after that, and then he came up again and we hit the sack and it was perfect. From there on we were a thing. For the next month or so I would finish my last trick around six in the morning, go to sleep, and wake up when he came pounding on my door at noon or so. Then we went back to bed for a while or took in a show and had dinner out. Once in a great while I cooked something in the apartment. Then, after dinner, off I went to Lexington to do some good honest work.

During that time we didn't plan. In the kind of life we were leading you didn't think about tomorrow and you tried your best to forget all your yesterdays. We had each day as it came, and that was usually enough to make up for the lack of a past and a future. But the more we saw of each other the more we fell in love, and the more we loved each other the more we got to thinking about what was coming up for us. He was the first to put words to the tune.

"This is good, Liz. We ought to make a steady thing out of it."

"You want to move in? I invited you."

"That's not what I mean."

"How else can it get steadier than it is? You come over every day, Phil. It's pretty steady already, isn't it?"

He lit a cigarette and took a deep drag on it. "Honey," he said, "you know what I mean. As long as you're hustling and I'm doing what I'm doing we don't have much of a chance. It never works that way. I know people who tried. It doesn't work."

"So?"

"So nothing. Forget it."

I knew he had more to say so I shut up and let him say it. He took a few more puffs on the cigarette, then ground it out in an ashtray. "I mean we ought to get out," he said. "Out of the rackets. I get a job and you get a job and we make babies. That kind of thing. We go nice and square and try to be people again."

I looked at him.

"Forget I said it," he muttered. "It's a nutty idea."

"I think it sounds pretty good."

"You do?"

"Uh-huh," I said. "I think it sounds pretty good. I think we're going to try it."

"It's long odds, Liz."

"The longest," I agreed. "But I always liked the long shots. Now come to bed and make me happy."

The odds were very long. Getting out of the business was no problem at all. Neither of us worked for a boss who was aching to keep us on the string. We weren't that valuable. Getting out was easy; it was staying out that got rough.

Very rough.

I had a lot of money saved. We moved out of Manhattan to a cheap three-room apartment in Brooklyn Heights and furnished it second-hand so we still had some dough left over to hold us while we looked around for work. The dough came to almost two grand. It was gone pretty soon. When you're used to fairly high living it's not easy to come down.

When you're used to the rackets it is even harder to get a

job. For one thing, what the hell could I do? The only experience I ever had was flat on my back. That can get you plenty of work, but not honest work. And that was the only kind I was interested in. I couldn't type and I couldn't take dictation, and I had a lousy telephone voice. That made things difficult.

It was even harder for Phil. He had done a bit in the pokey once before for passing bad checks and he'd been picked up by the fuzz plenty of times. He could have handled plenty of jobs, but getting hired was next to impossible. When he did land a job driving a truck, he got bounced when the guy who hired him found out he had a record. After that he was too discouraged to try.

We could have made it, I think. We could have found jobs eventually if we hadn't had a racket cushion to fall back on. But the cushion was there and it was a nice soft one.

I got a job washing dishes and managed to work my way up to slinging hash. I put in forty-five hours a week at a hot buck an hour. That gave me as much as three cheap tricks would bring me and when I got home my feet were killing me from all the standing up. I was knocking down less in a week than I earned in a day and I was working like a Turk for it.

How much of that can a person stand?

One day, for the hell of it, Phil put five bucks on a very long shot that happened to come home and pay $52.50 for a deuce. He couldn't earn that much in a month. When things like that happen you don't see too many roses on the straight and narrow path.

"Liz—"

"I know, honey."

"Liz, we can't go on like this. We spend more than we earn and it was all your money. And you've been killing yourself in that stinking beanery."

"What else can we do?"

"Nothing. Forget it."

But we both knew damned well what else we could do. We could set me up in business and live high again. But neither of us was willing to mention it. We were the gold dust twins out to go straight and narrow. Hustling was a dirty word.

He got another job and lost it. Then he got another one and quit when the foreman gave him a pain. I missed work one day and didn't bother going back. We just weren't built for honest work. You get that way after you spend your time on the hip side of the street. Dishonest dollars we could make. Not honest ones.

It's corny but I have to say it. We still had each other. We were still together, and we still made each other happy in bed and out, and we felt a lot cleaner inside than ever before in our lives. We weren't married, by the way—that would have been a little bit too square for a couple of sharpies like us. If what we had wasn't enough without a piece of paper and a ring, then it wasn't anything at all. But we were man and wife, ring or no, and we had each other, and maybe it should have been enough.

It wasn't.

Yeah, you guessed it. I turned a trick. I went out one day and walked around Brooklyn and let myself get picked up and taken to a hotel room. I felt like a pig when it was over, but we needed the money. I didn't tell Phil how I got it. I think he knew right off the bat, but I didn't tell him and he didn't ask and we let it lie.

And I turned another trick.

It was a funny way to hustle. I wasn't trying to make a lot of money, just enough to get by on. I'd take on one or two guys a day, no more than that, and I'd only play it straight. The weirdo stuff was out completely.

And, bit by bit, our "marriage" went quietly to hell. It was a downhill glide and it took a long time coming, but every damned day knocked us a little bit farther apart. Phil started hitting the sauce pretty heavily—hell, he was drinking like a fish—and we dropped the *let's pretend we don't know where the bread's coming from* routine. I was hustling and I was supporting him. We faced up to it.

The hell of the whole bit is that if Phil had been a rat or something we could have worked it out. Worked it out? We could have lasted, let me put it that way. He would have done whatever he wanted and I would have hustled my tail off for him and the two of us would have been as happy together as any whore and pimp can be. But it didn't work that way.

He was too good a person. He let me earn my living hustling and he took the money I gave him, but he had a conscience. He felt bad about it. He took it but he didn't like it, and that made the breakup a sure thing. I suppose it wouldn't take the greatest psychiatrist in the world to figure out why everything fell apart. I was keeping him and he didn't want to be kept. And, for that matter, I didn't want to hustle. The result was that we started hating each other. There was nothing else that could have happened. We were all loused up inside, and we took it out by hating each other. We were in love but we were also in hate. That sort of combination doesn't make for a fine and lasting life.

Once in a while, when he was more drunk than usual he would hit me. Once in a while, when I was in a bitchy mood, I would tell him he was worse than a pimp. The once-in-a-whiles started coming closer and closer together. One time he disappeared on a bat and didn't come home for a week. Then he walked in smelling of another woman. So I got even by working my tail off for a week, taking on all comers. Then, like a bitch, I came home and gave Phil a play-by-play summary of the whole business.

We weren't exactly a couple straight out of the pages of the *Saturday Evening Post*. And, less than a year from the day we started living together, we were no longer any kind of a couple. I moved back into a little apartment a block from my old place and Phil disappeared. It ended. Period. End of report.

I still think about it and I will always think about it. I'm a whore again and Phil, I've recently heard, is a small timer in the rackets, currently doing a stretch in Dannemora. But for a little while there we were people. Real people. Nice, straight, square, honest people.

I wish it could have lasted. I think I would have done anything in the world just so it could have worked itself out. I sit around every once in a while and think about what it might have been—steady jobs, a television set, beer in the fridge, a baby. Then another baby, and maybe a house somewhere out in Queens, and then living together and getting old and watching the kids grow up.

I could have had that—

Oh, the hell I could. Let's not kid ourselves. I was a whore without guts enough to change. It's all I ever was and all I'll ever be—a woman who lays like a rug and gets paid for it, because it's the easy way out.

Liz Crowley, this is your life. And you can have it.

BACK TO THE STREET . . .

When Phil and I fell apart I wasn't a kid any more. I was twenty-five and I looked older. Don't get me wrong—I wasn't coming apart at the seams. I still had my shape and I still had a face that would let a clock go right on running. But seventeen I wasn't, and I found something out. The years make a difference.

A big difference. Before I hooked up with Phil Notaro, my scene was twenty-dollar tricks in bars on Lexington Avenue. Toward the end of the year with Phil, when I started turning a trick or two a day, it was street pick-ups. But that was only because I wasn't trying to make big money. When we broke up and I flew solo again I figured on going straight back to Lexington. I got a surprise.

I tried hustling one place and it didn't work too well. The other chicks in the bar were like children, every damn one of them younger than I was. I felt like somebody's grandmother. And the tricks must have felt the same way about me. I didn't do a hell of a lot of trade. I wasn't going hungry, but it was a long ways from how it used to be.

"Liz," the bartender said one night, "it might be a good idea if you took your business some place else."

"What are you talking about?"

He was a big sad-eyed guy and he talked as though it was hurting him to move his lips. "Some people don't want you around, Liz. It's not my idea, believe me. I got the word and I'm supposed to pass it on to you. From where I sit, you ought to listen."

There was a mirror behind the bar and I looked into it and saw myself. Hell, I wasn't a bad-looking woman. "I suppose I lower the tone of the joint. Is that it?"

"Liz, as far as I'm concerned you could stay here forever. But—"

"But I don't pay my freight," I said. "The others look better than I do and their breasts bounce better. I get the message. I'll leave quietly, sweetheart."

I got up and headed for the door. I was burning but there was no one in particular that I was mad at. The bartender was passing on information. The owners were only looking out for their own. The years were the only thing to be mad at. And hating time doesn't do much good.

"Liz—" The bartender's voice sounded guilty and regretful. I turned around.

"I'm sorry, Liz." His eyes looked hurt. He'd had to do something that went against the grain.

He wasn't the only one who was sorry.

*   *   *

The bars were out and so were the houses. I could have hooked up with a pimp but I didn't want to. That left the street. But it took me a little while to get up my nerve.

You've got to understand about the street. When you're on the street you've hit the bottom, in a sense. You can make decent money and you can work when you want to work, but you're only a cheap streetwalker and it hurts to look in the mirror. You're the first one arrested when the heat comes on. You're a doormat for every trick you take on. A trick can have a little respect for a house girl or a bar pick-up, but every trick in the world thinks of a streetwalker as a piece of dirt. It took a little thinking about it before I was ready to walk the streets. I had to get myself used to the idea.

So I got used to the idea. When you're a whore you can get used to almost anything. I thought about it and I smoked a few sticks for courage and away we went. I walked around on Eighth Avenue and I let my tricks take me to a hotel in the neighborhood. I think the hotel made more money on me the first two nights than I did.

I had troubles, too. Eighth Avenue was one hell of a street at the time. The girls weren't subtle. They couldn't afford to be because the competition was something fierce. If a man walked down Eighth Avenue after midnight he didn't have a chance. Hustlers would latch onto his arm and start messing around and tell him what a hot time they would show him. They got a lot of business that way, but I just couldn't get used to that sort of approach. I had always waited for the men to come to me. It seemed dirty and cheap to have to do the approaching myself.

But, like everything else, I got used to it. It took a long time, but if you pass me late at night nowadays I'll have my hooks into you before you know what's going on. I'm sharper now.

It was tougher then. The pickings were worse than slim, and on my second night on the street I made a hot twenty bucks. That was bad enough, but about a week later I played out a scene that damn near finished the whole routine. It got me off the streets, if nothing else. It was a long time before I worked the Avenue again.

Kids are usually the best tricks. They pay less and they try to haggle a lot of the time, but generally a young guy is easy work and easy money. There's a reason for this.

When an older guy goes to a hustler it's quite often because he wants something special. With a kid, it's usually because he never had a woman before, or hasn't had many, and he wants to find out what it's all about. Maybe he's worried, or maybe he's scared, or maybe he just never managed to get taken care of before and he wants to quit being a virgin. When it's something like that, a hustler has a good deal. For one thing, she just turns a straight trick. For another, a young kid with no experience doesn't take very long to finish what he starts. Remember, time is money. The less time you have to spend with a trick, the more time you have for yourself.

That's why I was happy when the five of them picked me up. They were about seventeen or eighteen, all dressed alike in dungarees and black leather jackets. It's the standard juvenile delinquent uniform, but a lot of plain ordinary kids dress the part. It's a stage they go through. In grammar school they try to dress like cowboys and in high school they try to dress like hoods. Then they grow up and try to dress like advertising men.

The big one talked. "How about it? You want to take on the five of us?"

"Sure," I said. "I'll show you a good time, guys. I'm pretty fine stuff."

"Sure you are. How much do you get?"

"Ten," I said.

"For the five of us? That's two bucks apiece."

"Ten each," I said. "That makes fifty. Take it or leave it."

"I don't know," the big one said. "A lot of bread. What do you think, Eddie? Is she worth it?"

Eddie was the one with glasses and a runny nose. I felt like handing him a handkerchief. But Eddie was also the eager type, and he said ten was a lot of money but I was probably worth it.

"I dunno," the big one said. "You gonna be good to us?"

"The best you ever had," I said. *The only one you ever had,* I thought to myself.

"We vote then," the big one said. He had arms like a leg of lamb. "Eddie?"

Eddie voted for me.

"Jim?"

"Too much money." Jim was fat and sloppy. He had pimples.

"Zig?"

"I can swing ten." Zig was the beanpole type. He kept looking at my breasts.

"Lennie?"

"I'm in."

"Three to one," the big one said. "I don't even have to vote. It looks like you're gonna make yourself a fast fifty skins, sweetheart. Let's get going so you can earn it."

I told them I had a hotel to take them to, and they told me what I could do with my hotel. "We got a club-room," Lennie said. "No rent to pay if we go to our own club."

It was a cellar club on 56th Street way over on the West Side. My heroes were too cheap to spring for a cab so we walked. It was a hell of a walk, but fifty bucks is nice money. And the going had been slow lately. I went to the club, a room in a basement furnished with a broken-down sofa and a worn-out record player and a couple of chairs. The couch, needless to say, was for me.

The big guy, whose name I never did manage to catch, gave me ten five-dollar bills. I put them in the billfold I carried and wrapped it up in my clothes. Then the party started.

It wasn't too bad. Eddie managed to go first and he was sort of a nice guy in a simple kind of a way. He had a little trouble getting there but it went fast once it got going. Then it was Jim's turn, the fat sloppy one with the pimples who thought ten bucks was more than I was worth. He was all set on getting his money's worth and he gave me a hard time. Maybe he read

a book on perversion or something. Whatever it was he had
fancy ideas.

Then Zig and Lennie. Straight tricks again, nothing to it.
Then the big lug and things got rough. It was a straight trick
with a slight added attraction. He liked to hurt a girl a little.
He pinched me and bit me and slapped me around and it hurt.

When he finished with me I got dressed and started for the
door. But it wasn't that easy, because Mr. Big was standing in
front of it with his arms folded across his chest. I waited for
him to get out of the way. It began to look as though I was
going to have a long wait.

"The money," he said, his face mean and hard.

I didn't get it.

"The money," he repeated. "This ain't a charity. You want to
get out of here, you better hand over the fifty."

"I'm not a charity myself. I did everything you wanted me
to do, didn't I?"

"So what?" He had an ugly smile on his face. "We don't pay
for it," he said. "That's for the suckers. We find something we
want and we take it. Just be glad we aren't marking you up a
little."

I was getting mad. "I'm keeping that dough," I said. "You
can't stop me!"

That's what I thought. Because the next thing I knew a fist
exploded in my stomach and my guts turned inside out. Then
he gave me a punch in the breast and I sagged. It hurt like sixty.
I was afraid he was going to beat me to death.

He picked me up off the floor and started slapping me

across the face. Then I got another punch in the breast and I went down moaning like a cat with its guts cut open. I just lay there blubbering while he went through my billfold and took the fifty, plus fifteen bucks of my own.

"A dividend," he said. "That's nice."

They pushed me outside and left me there. I wanted to get away but I couldn't move. I finally found a hack to drive me home. When we got to my place I didn't have any money, so I made him wait while I went upstairs for my purse. After he drove away, I dragged myself back upstairs and collapsed on the bed.

That was the end of the street for the time being. I was scared stiff, to tell you the truth. Those kids were animals—especially the big one. I think he could have killed me and never given a good hoot in hell. Kids are like that these days—wolves traveling in wolf packs. We were tough in the Kitchen but we were human beings. These kids weren't human at all.

There was another way to play it besides streetwalking. Not much different, but it eliminated my being on Eighth Avenue, which was fine with me. It's called working cars. I don't know if it goes on anywhere in the world outside of New York and London, so maybe I ought to explain it.

The bit goes like this: you walk along the street, any street, and you go up to the cars that are waiting for a light. If there's a guy alone in the car and he looks like a possible trick you ask him for a lift. If he says no, then the hell with him. If he says yes, you get into the front seat with him and show a little leg.

Generally the guy gets the message right away and figures out you are a hustler. Some marks are a little bit denser than others and it takes more work. Then you sort of hint around, by telling him you don't have any special place in mind when he asks you where you're going. If he's interested, you fix a price. If he's not, you get out and look around for somebody else. When you find a trick it gets simple. You can take care of him in the car or in a hotel or even in your own apartment. That part is no problem at all.

The advantage is that you can do it anywhere and you're not limited to the Avenue. On top of that, you get a lot of guys who weren't looking for a whore to begin with but who get the idea when they've got you in the car with them. The money could be worse, too.

I got to see a lot of New York that way. One day I'd work cars on the East Side and the next day I'd be over on upper Broadway. Or one guy would give me a lift, then park on a quiet street and give the back seat a workout. He'd drop me off and I'd pick up my customer on the nearest corner. It didn't get dull. A little cramped, maybe, because cars weren't built for that sort of thing. There was one little episode in a sports car that was sort of a nightmare. But it could have been worse. Every once in a while something funny would happen and brighten my whole day. You see, picking cars at random like that you wind up with a lot of guys who just aren't in the market for a woman. One time I wound up in a car with a minister who wanted to save my soul when he found out what my pitch was. Another time was even better. The guy I hitched a ride with turned out to be a fag. He couldn't have been less interested in what I had to offer.

Yeah, I got my laughs. But, well, let's face it—it stank. All across the board it stank. I would get pretty depressed now and then and many times I thought about suicide to end the whole rotten mess. If I'd had the guts I probably would have killed myself. But pot and gin got me through. A couple sticks of pot and a couple belts of gin and things got a little rosier. I didn't walk around singing at the top of my lungs, but I kept myself from turning on the gas and sticking my head in the oven.

Then, one day when I was quietly stoned out of my head on four sticks and half a pint of juice, I did a real bright thing. I must have been high as a kite.

I was on Sixth Avenue at the corner of Eighth Street in the Village. It was a little after midnight and I was very high and feeling no pain. A car stopped at the signal and I went into my routine. The driver was a good-looking guy in his mid-thirties—a solid-citizen type. I didn't even wait for an invitation, just opened the door and hopped in next to him.

"I want a ride," I announced.

"Where to?"

"Wherever you're going," I said. "And you can do whatever kind of driving you want."

He said something that I didn't catch and I relaxed in the

seat. I felt great. The car was grooving along and I was way up on top of the world. I felt like singing.

"How much, honey?"

"Ten," I said. "Ten little dollars for anything you want to do. I'm cool as ice and hot as fire. I sing and I swing, lover. I'm good as gold, indeed I am."

"Sure," he said, giving me a strange grin.

I looked out the window. We weren't on Sixth Avenue any more and I wasn't too sure just where we were. The neighborhood didn't look familiar. "Park anywhere," I told my trick. "Unless you want to go to a hotel. I'd just as soon if you want. I know a good hotel."

"No hotel, honey."

"The car, then? This is a good place to park if you want."

"Not the car."

"Where, then? Tell me, lover. Where you taking me?"

His voice was tired. "The police station," he said. "You're under arrest, sweetheart."

I Take a Fall . . .

I was panicked. For eight years I managed to stay out of the can and now I was walking straight into it. All the cars in the world and I had to pick a cop!

"Hold on," I said. "Maybe we can work a deal."

He shook his head. "No deal."

"I can pay off, man. Any payoff you name. Cash or trade or both. I just want to stay out of the tank."

He looked me over and I felt naked. "Sorry," he said. "Hell, you're the type of broad we *have* to pick up. You don't work for anybody and you don't even have the brains to stick to the street. You're the kind of hustler who louses thing up for everybody. You bother some guy who isn't interested and he phones in a complaint. It makes the squad look bad. It makes the whole force look bad."

It wasn't enough he was arresting me. I had to get a lecture in the bargain because I made his little bunch of cops look bad. I felt like belting him.

"Five hundred dollars. I've got five hundred bucks in my room and it's all yours if you don't turn me in. Isn't that enough?"

"Plenty," he said. "But no deal."

He didn't waste any time. He drove straight to the station and there I was. I didn't even bother arguing or trying to deal. It was useless. I was busted and there was no way out. I stood there feeling filthy while they booked me and printed me and went through all the nonsense they go through. I knew what to expect—I knew plenty of girls who had taken falls before. But knowing what it was going to be like and going through it, turned out to be two entirely different things. I didn't think I could stand it. But I did. You'd be surprised how much a person can stand.

The cute part of it is that the Woman's House of Detention is on the corner of Sixth and Greenwich Avenues in the Village just a couple of blocks from where the fuzz picked me up in the first place. He could have dropped me off there and saved himself some driving. But I got there anyhow. And it stank. Believe me, it stank out loud. It's a big stone building that looks like a prison. Which is just what it is.

"Crowley?"

The matron looked like a schoolteacher with muscles. I answered when she called my name and she made me strip down. She was looking for concealed narcotics, I suppose. I didn't have any needle marks and I obviously wasn't a user but that didn't matter a damn to her. She gave me a good searching. I don't have to tell you what cute places she picked to look for junk.

The clothes she gave me to put on were as gray as the walls.

No hooks, no belt—I might try to kill myself, and the law doesn't want anybody doing that. The law does its own killing.

I landed in a cell with two other broads. One was as drunk as a lord and sloppy as a pig. She must have been fifty and she was in for hustling. A man would have to be pretty hard up to give her a nod. But you never can tell. I hear there are some men who prefer any old wreck of a prostitute to nice fresh stuff. I'm damned if I can see why, but that's what they tell me.

The other one was a militant dyke, if you know what I mean. Not the type that wants to keep you company but the type who is going to get you whether you like it or not. She was in for hustling, too, and she planned to make the most of it. Since she had a choice between fatso and me, I was elected. I wanted her about as much as I wanted false teeth, but after she told me what she was going to do to me if I didn't come across, I gave her what she wanted. It was just another trick. My pay in this case was being let alone afterwards.

For a week they just left us there. That's the beauty of New York—they arrest you for something carrying a thirty-day sentence if they convict you, and it's sixty days before you get to court. That's why I pleaded guilty when they gave me the chance. I couldn't raise bail, and if I stuck around for a trial I would be out of work for a year. Besides, I figured I had a damn good chance of getting a suspension. I was lucky—it was my first arrest. You rarely have to do a bit on your first fall. Not for disorderly conduct, which was the charge. Incidentally, that's the usual charge in New York. In order to get you for prostitution they have to be able to prove that you've exposed yourself intimately in return for money. Disorderly conduct means whatever they want it to mean. It's convenient for them.

So I sweated out a week while they got ready to bring me up before the judge, handling the dyke when I had to and taking it easy the rest of the time. It wasn't fun but it wasn't quite as lousy as I thought it would be. The food was almost edible and the mattress didn't have many bugs.

And then it was time for sentencing.

The judge was a fat old clown with thick glasses and a high squeaky voice. He looked like somebody's old uncle. I thought at first it was a break because he looked like an easy judge, one that wouldn't be likely to hand out stiff sentences. Which goes to show you can't tell anything from the way a person looks. He was a rat.

"Miss Crowley?"

"Yes, Your Honor." I was playing it by the books. I could afford to be nice—it wouldn't kill me and it might keep me out of jail. I should have saved my breath.

"You've pleaded guilty to disorderly conduct," he said. "You have committed a crime against society and a crime against God."

That convinced me. As soon as they start talking that way you might as well go shoot yourself.

"You're a disgrace to this city, Miss Crowley. I don't for the life of me understand how an attractive woman can sink so deep into the mire of sinfulness. There are men who condone prostitution. There are men who think women of your ilk should be permitted to ply your disgusting and dishonest trade. I have never found myself in agreement with these men."

And then I got the message. The old boy was on the take— that's why I was getting such a deep message. For the right people he was the softest touch in the world. To make up for that, he was the hardest judge around if you didn't have the right connections. And I didn't.

Now he was trying to look good. The broads who had the fix in would get suspended sentences and I would get a rap to make up for their good luck. The old boy had to balance things out, damn him. He picked up my record and stared at the sheet of paper through those thick glasses of his until I thought the paper would catch fire.

"This is your first offense, I see." I thought maybe I was wrong and he was going to take that into consideration. It was a thought.

"There is a practice of granting suspended sentences to first offenders," he said. "It is a practice of which I have always disapproved. In my opinion, a first offender ought to be penalized instantly and mercilessly. This will serve both to teach a lesson and to set an example."

Get it? I was going to be an example. Yeah.

"Perhaps you are new to the vicious trade of prostitution, Miss Crowley. In that case this sentence may save you from further arrests and sentences. I hereby sentence you to sixty days' imprisonment."

Sixty days for a first fall. Nice.

"Have you anything to say, Miss Crowley?" I looked at him,

the little dried up powderpuff with the squeaky little voice. And I had something to say but not what he was expecting. I had a few words to say and they weren't *I love you.* The words were tough and to the point.

"I must have misunderstood you," he said. "Would you repeat that, please?"

It meant another bit for contempt but I just did not happen to give a damn. I repeated it loud and clear. There wasn't a person in the courtroom who missed it.

The gavel banged. "Let's make that ninety days, shall we? Thirty days additional for contempt of court. Next case, please."

Bright it wasn't but I didn't care. It was worth thirty more days to tell him what I thought of him. And if you can do sixty days you can do ninety. Doing time isn't as hard as it's cracked up to be. You just sit there and rot and count the goddamned days.

So I sat and rotted and counted days. I was back in the House of Detention but this time I was in a cell block with girls who had already been sentenced. There were a lot of us. The girl I was in with was doing a year and a day for possession of heroin. She was a junkie, and the geniuses who run New York seem to think that the way to cure a junkie is to throw her in the can. They are so damned stupid it's a panic. My cellmate had her shot a day. A guard brought it to her. It cost her but she didn't have any trouble getting it. She'd leave the can as hooked as the day she walked in.

Our cell even had a window, which was something. You

know what we used to do? This will kill you. We would stand at the window and call out to anybody who passed by. We'd shout nasty things and proposition men. I don't know what the hell was the kick in it, but after I was there for a few days I found myself doing it, too. I think it's because when you're in the can, any contact with the rest of the world is better than none. By yelling to guys on the street we managed to realize that there was really a world out there. You have to do that or you think that there's nothing at all beyond those stone walls.

My cellmate finished her bit before I did. I remember her very well, even though I never did run into her again. She was a Negro girl and she must have been very pretty before the needle got to her. She was still all right but heroin was starting to poison her system and turn her into a ghost. She wasn't a criminal except for her habit. She was a married woman with a family. Her husband was also a junkie and their last kid had been born with what they call a congenital habit.

She had a real life, huh? I think it's people like her that keep me going. Every once in a while I get in these *let's feel sorry for poor little Liz* moods, and it takes remembering girls like her to bring me out of it. I've got it soft compared to a batch of gals I've known.

The gal who took her place was in for the same thing I was. In a few ways she was a lot like me. She was a Polack from the lower East Side instead of a mick from the Kitchen and she was a year or two younger than me, but outside of that we were a lot alike. We even got sent up by the same judge.

Her name was Carla Metakowski and she was my height,

with my build and my coloring. She had the saddest eyes I ever saw in my life and she spent at least half her life in tears. She cried all day and half the night. I wondered when her eyes were going to dry up. She would cry even if she didn't have a thing in the world to cry about. It was just the way she was and she couldn't help it.

When she wasn't crying, we talked. She was even in the can for the same reason I was—she was outlawing it and didn't have any connections. That was one of the things she cried about all the time. It seems her pimp had tossed her out on her ear and she had no place to go.

Her pimp, oddly enough, was a Negro. There are two reasons why a white girl will occasionally take on a Negro pimp. For one thing, it makes a prostitute feel better, because that makes him lower socially than she is, which is the main reason for having a pimp in the first place. Besides that, it's one sure way a Negro can make a decent living. You can thank the brilliant setup in this country for that part of it. A spade cat without an education—or even with one—has a choice between sweeping floors at forty bucks a week or living off women at closer to a grand a week. Which would you pick?

"It's nice uptown," Carla used to tell me. "I never would of left except he got mad at me and threw me out." She never did mention why he got mad. I didn't ask. I make it a point not to ask people things. They tell me if they want to.

"How's it nice there?"

"The cops don't bother you," she said. "And you get treated nice and you make nice money. Much nicer than downtown."

"You mean your pimp makes nice money."

"What's the difference?" I thought she was going to start bawling again but she surprised me and smiled instead. "So he gets the money. I get taken care of and everything's fine. He takes me out to dinner more than any of the other ones, too."

"Other ones?"

"He had seven girls," she said. "But I was his favorite. He always told me I was his favorite and he only kept the others so that he would have more money for me and him to live on. You see, we were going to go away from there when he had enough money and then we would open up a store in a little town and live together and have babies. But he got mad at me and threw me out."

Did you catch that? He had seven girls working for him, and each one of them believed she was his one and only. I almost laughed when she gave me that crap about how they were going to buy a store and get married and soon. Then I remembered the line Johnny had handed me and I decided there was nothing to laugh about. Whores like us think we know it all, but when you come right down to it we have one hell of a lot of blind spots.

The time in jail slowly passed. Ninety days is three months, and three months is a quarter of a year. If you estimate that a person lives to be seventy, ninety days in jail is something like one/280th of your life. I figured it out once. Imagine spending that much of your life in jail. Hell, think of the millions of people who draw five-year bits. Five years is supposed to be a short fall. But it's one-fourteenth of a life.

When I thought like that it made the ninety days go a little faster. Towards the end it got impossible to wait any more. Every day I thought, *Well, one less day to go.* And the days took so damn long to pass it was driving me nuts. The last week, of course, was the worst. I drove poor Carla half nutty herself the way I paced the floor. Up and down, back and forth—I just kept walking and waiting. I thought to myself what a dope I was—if I hadn't talked back to the judge I'd have gotten out a whole month earlier. You can bet I'd never pull a routine like that again.

As a matter of fact, you can bet I'll never get busted again. And if I do, I won't serve time. I'll die first. It's the waiting that's the worst part of it. Maybe somebody in for life has it easier. They don't have to wait and wait and wait to get out.

Oh, they don't have it so easy, I guess. They have to wait the same way.

They have to wait to die.

When they let me out it was the most beautiful day of my life. I walked out the door and there was a world out there, a big and beautiful world. I was free. I was out. I was never going back.

I didn't know New York could look so beautiful. I walked over to Washington Square and looked at the grass. When you're in jail you get so you forget what grass looks like. It looked good to me.

Then I headed for the subway. And then a man was looking at me, smiling. "Hey, girlie," he called. "How about it?"

It was the same stinking, rotten world again.

Harlem Lights...

Lucian Gill was the neatest-looking man I ever met. His skin was the color of coffee with cream and his teeth were perfectly white and even. He was six feet tall, with a slender build and a steady way of walking. He dressed carefully in extremely conservative clothes. He wore suits instead of sports jackets and the suits were either gray flannel or neat pinstripes. He spoke quietly, gently, like a college professor or something like that. He always called me Elizabeth.

"I don't quite understand you, Elizabeth," he said when we met for the first time and I told him what I wanted. "You are an intelligent woman. You must realize that the relationship between a procurer and a prostitute is financially disastrous for the woman involved. It's one which works to her advantage only because she needs to satisfy her personal psychological demands. Yet you seem to want the relationship without the emotional satisfaction. I don't understand."

I didn't understand, either. I didn't understand what the hell he was saying. The words got in my way there for a minute, but when he got them translated back into English I was on my feet again. He wanted to know why I was trying to get into his stable without being in love with him or anything. So I told him.

"I took a fall, Lucian. I did ninety days. You ever been in prison?"

He shook his head. The expression on his face said he had no desire to be in prison. Ever.

"Ninety days, Lucian. It could be worse. It probably will be worse next time around. I don't want to chance it."

"The fix—"

"—stinks outside of Harlem. I checked. I asked around. The heat is hot as hell for the time being, unless you've got tight connections that go right to the top. It may last like that. I can't afford to go it alone. I don't want to take the chance of another fall."

"I see."

"So I figured an uptown deal would be the best bet for me. I don't care about the money, to tell you the truth. You can take all of it and I won't put up a kick. Just so I have enough to live on, that's all I care about. A good apartment and a food allowance and protection. That's enough for me."

"That's simple enough," he said. "You'd have to live uptown, of course."

"I don't mind. Oh, and one thing more. If I want to cut out and go it alone I don't want any arguments. Fair enough?"

He nodded, smiling gently. "And love, Elizabeth? That's a woman's privilege in this sort of arrangement, you know. Will you want me to make love to you?"

"I don't need it," I said, "and you got enough broads to take care of. I might as well save all I got for the paying customers."

You can call me a damn fool if you want. I was putting myself in a box where I did all the work and didn't wind up with a nickel. But I didn't care. In Lucian's stable I wouldn't have any worries about the fuzz. I would get a good apartment and good clothes—the word was out that Lucian Gill took a hell of a lot better care of the broads in his stable than the rest of the pimps around. As for saving money, it doesn't do you a hell of a lot of good when the cops break down the door. Protection was more important to me than a bank account. I didn't want to see the inside of another jail again. That was pretty big with me at the time. I got nervous thinking about jails. Once was enough.

And when you are in Harlem you are safe. The police don't make too much trouble up there. And so it made things nice for me. I relaxed completely and took it nice and easy. Lucian set me up in an apartment, one of eight in a four-story brownstone he owned on 128th Street near St. Nicholas. Every apartment in the building was rented to one of Lucian's girls. The girls didn't fight among themselves. It was nice and cozy.

I didn't have any trouble getting in solid with Lucian's girls. As soon as they found out I wasn't interested in taking Lucian to bed, they loved me like sisters. The way they saw it, I was putting money in their pot and not taking out anything in return. So I had a home and friendly neighbors. That ought to count for something.

Of the seven other girls, three were white and four were

Negro. They ranged in age from Millie, a spade chick three years older than me, to Angela, a seventeen-year-old from wop Harlem. The eight of us made quite a family. A customer could get just about anything he wanted in that one brownstone. It wasn't run like an ordinary house, but I suppose it added up to the same thing the way we all lived together.

I got particularly friendly with Angela. She had eyes like saucers and breasts like watermelons. Her hair was jet black and she never cut it. It was almost to her waist when I met her. She was one hell of a beautiful girl. In a way, she reminded me of me—I mean, she was seventeen, the same age as I was when I started in the business. She had it different at home, though. Her parents were the religious fanatic type. They tried to keep her on a leash. Once the leash broke she was gone for good.

We used to sit and talk a lot. It would go something like this:

"I'm so lucky, Liz. I'm in love with Lucian and he's in love with me. It's perfect."

"Sure, Angie."

"He's the sweetest guy, Liz. He's nice to me and so cultured and everything. I'm lucky."

"You're one hell of a lucky girl, kid."

"I'll tell you something, Liz. I was supposed to keep it a secret but it's all right to tell you because you and Lucian never go to bed together. I'm his favorite one, Liz. He goes with me more than the others and he likes me better. How about that, huh?"

Was there ever a whore in the world who believed that her

pimp liked another girl better than her? If there was I never met her. I didn't have the heart to put Angie hip, though. Besides, she wouldn't believe me in a million years.

"You know why I do it, Liz?"

"Tell me, Angie."

"Not just because of Lucian," she said. "I love him, but even without him I'd still be a hustler. It's all because of the first time I let a boy do it to me. You know how it was?"

"How?"

"Perfect," Angela said. "Perfect and sweet as milk and honey, all the way. And you want to know something? It's always like that, Liz. Maybe I'm nuts or something. Maybe I ought to see one of those doctors who looks at your head and tells you what's wrong with you. But every time I go to bed with a man I love it. I love it so much I could scream. Every single time!"

It was a new one on me. But there was one thing for sure. Little Angie was in the right business.

"Baby," Ronnie said to me, "you just the wrong color for a hustler. You know that?"

She was a beautiful girl, deep nut-brown skin, perfect pear-shaped breasts. I listened to what she had to say.

"You just don't know," she said. "These cats come uptown and they don't want a fay chick." *Fay* means white in Harlem. It comes from *ofay,* which is pig Latin for foe. "They want something fresh out of the jungle. You want to know why?"

I waited.

"They think it's something special," she said. "They look at the skin and they think there's something different going on inside it. You know the bit. We're supposed to be hotter and better at it and more passionate and all the rest of it. Baby, they are *so* wrong. You know what I did the other night? Dig— you'll get a bang out of this. This guy came to me, you know, and I could see right off he was one of the idiots who like to hear jungle drums when they score with a chick. He was sure I was going to be hotter than fire. You know what I did?"

I shook my head.

"Well, I was very cool, baby. I played the little games he wanted me to play and then when he was ready to rock and roll I just stretched out on that bed like a corpse. There he was, working away like a madman, and there I was just cooling it and tuning in on my own private thoughts. You better believe it was funny, baby. He's going crazy, heating himself up and I'm like I'm dead. He could have had a better time in the morgue."

"Was he mad?"

She laughed. "Baby, that is the whole point! Mad? He was the happiest guy in the world, baby. He couldn't stop telling me how great I was. You know how he put it? *You little colored gals sure know how to set a man afire.* Set him on fire? I was pouring water on him, baby. I was icing him down!"

She stopped to light a cigarette. "That's why, baby, I'm lucky I'm Negro. You could have switched your tail off for this cat and he woulda thought he was missing something. You see how unlucky you are?"

I thought about it. "Look," I said, "next trick I get, I'll tell him I'm really passing."

Ronnie and I laughed our heads off over that one.

I stayed two years at Lucian's. Maybe it's funny, staying that long where I wasn't making money. I guess I was getting old or something. I could have moved any time but I didn't feel like pulling up and getting out. I was settled and life was easy so I stayed right where I was.

The same thing goes for the life itself, I suppose. When you're a whore for long enough, you stop thinking about getting out of the racket. Once you're there, that's what you are and it doesn't make much sense to change it. You just concentrate on doing a good job, turning your tricks and staying alive. When you think about getting out of the business, that's all you do—think. You never get around to doing anything about it.

I had a pretty good deal while I was with Lucian. My hours were easy, for one thing. I hardly ever took a guy on before midnight or after five. I had a day off any time I wanted it. I could turn a trick down if I didn't like his looks. Lucian was decent that way. The way he looked at it, I was getting a rotten deal. He made it up to me by being a good guy about other things. I had damn near everything but a pension plan. On my end of it, I was careful not to take advantage of him. I hardly ever turned down a trick, even specialty stuff. The only thing I wouldn't handle was a beating. But Millie was always available for that type of scene. I think she got a kick out of being beaten up. There are girls like that.

I got a lot of calls for specialty stuff uptown. When a white man goes to Harlem to live it up it's like Ronnie said—he's looking for a change. He wants excitement, something he can't get at home. When you come right down to it, of course, he's not getting anything different—nothing he couldn't get anywhere else in the world. But they never figure that part out.

One thing we got a lot of calls for was a lesbo routine. There is something about the idea of a spade chick and a white chick in bed together that seems to get a lot of men all worked up. I don't know why this is, but it is. To me it's the same as anything else.

For a deal like that we would get twenty-five bucks apiece. My general price at Lucian's was fifteen for a straight trick and on up for something special. Once in a great while there would be a guy who wanted to spend the whole night. When that happened we would haggle over the price. It was usually around fifty dollars.

Living in Harlem was okay most of the time. I used to go for long walks in the daytime, just wandering around and looking at what was happening. It was fun, but bit by bit it started to get on my nerves. Not that anybody ever bothered me. People were nice uptown. It was something else. It was that I didn't have to live there and they did. There was no place else for them to go. So I felt like an outsider, a phony. I don't know how much sense that makes but it was the way I felt. It's the main reason I left Harlem. Because I felt out of place.

I didn't belong there. I belonged where the whole thing got started in the first place—Hell's Kitchen. I was a Kitchen hustler with a Kitchen mind. It was something I couldn't shake loose and now it was time to go back.

When I told Lucian I thought he would be mad at me. He had agreed there would be no strings, but he was getting used to having me around. I was all ready for an argument and I was surprised when it didn't come.

"I'm surprised you have stayed this long in Harlem, Elizabeth." He smiled. "You've been a good girl. Our relationship has been both pleasant and profitable for me. I am sorry to see you go, but I will not try to hold you. You need not worry on that account."

"I got to go back downtown again, Lucian."

"I understand. You feel like a fish out of water here, don't you? It's perfectly understandable. But I thought you were worried about an arrest. Or aren't you scared any longer?"

"I'm still shook," I admitted. "I don't want to go back to the can. But the word is out that the heat's nothing like what it used to be."

"That's partly correct, Elizabeth. A person with a connection is invulnerable. But connections are difficult to come by."

I didn't say anything.

"I can help you," he said. "You'll be entirely on your own, but you'll have to turn in precisely half your take to a Mr.

Ralph Carter. He's an acquaintance of mine. I'll let him know your status and everything will be taken care of."

"That's swell of you, Lucian."

He smiled. "Carter owes me a favor. Now, if you will, I'd like you to do *me* a favor, Elizabeth."

"What?"

"I'd like you to go to bed with me. If you don't mind."

I was completely shook. Hell, he could have made it with me any time he wanted. But he had never asked before. Come to think of it, I must have been the first hustler in the history of the world who didn't go to bed once with her pimp.

"Sure," I said. "But—"

"But why do I want to all of a sudden?" He smiled again. "I don't know myself. But I'd like to if you don't mind."

"Sure," I said. "Anything you want."

I didn't know quite what to make of it. I started to peel off my clothes but he stopped me and led me to the double bed. Then he took me in his arms and kissed me. It was the first kiss in a long time—whores don't get kissed a hell of a lot. I liked it.

Slowly, gently, Lucian undressed me. I felt my body come alive for the first time in a long time. I was doing it not for money, not as a payoff, but because he wanted to and I wanted to. It made a difference. A big difference.

His hands were tender and I felt the excitement building inside of me. I began to breathe hard and this time the excitement was real, not an act put on for a trick. Our lovemaking was slow and thorough and it lasted a long time. When it was all over my heart was pounding. I could barely see. And then Lucian was drawing away from me, his eyes tender.

"Thank you," he said. "Thank you, Elizabeth."

For just a few hours the glow of our being together lasted and I didn't feel like a whore any more.

Ralph Carter was smooth as silk and tough as tempered steel. He was business all the way. God knows how many rackets he handled as fixer in one form or another. I know he took care of protection for two or three heavy floating dice games and a hell of a lot of prostitutes. The word was out that the pornography business paid off to him, as well. He was rolling in dough.

"Lucian says you're honest," he said. "You know the deal. You work Seventh Avenue between Fifty-first and Forty-seventh. No place else. If somebody hits you while you're walking around somewhere else, you don't know him. You hustle only where you're supposed to hustle."

He paused for breath. "You stay off the streets until one in the morning, two on Saturdays and Sundays. Otherwise you run into too many tourists. Got that?"

I told him that was fine.

"Don't turn tricks in your own pad. You get a room by the month on the West Side. Live some place else. Okay?"

"Okay."

"And you pay me half your take. I'll find out if you hold out. I always find out. Half, on the button, payable every Monday afternoon. Or you're dead."

HOME

Lucian had given me five hundred bucks as a going-away present. It may have been small in comparison to what I earned for him but he didn't have to give me a cent, so I think it was a damn nice thing for him to do. It paid my rent and it bought me some clothes. I was in business.

I took an apartment on West 73rd Street right off the park, a good-sized bedroom and a small living room with a kitchenette that was too small to think in. It came furnished and the furniture was decent stuff. But I figured it was about time I started living good. Thanks to Lucian, I was in a position to save up some dough. With enough money saved up I could even make a try at going straight.

My "office" was not quite so beautiful. It was in the Kitchen on West 47th Street, as I think I said before. One room—a real mess. My rent on 73rd Street was $100 a month and my rent on 47th was $150. There was a reason. I wasn't turning tricks on 73rd Street.

My landlord was entitled to maybe thirty bucks a month on the room. He got five times that for forgetting how I made my money. Part of what he got went to a fixer who made sure the rest of the world forgot what went on in his rooms. See how it works? Everything is like that. No matter what racket is going on, everybody has his hand out for a piece of it. And there's always some bastard on top getting rich out of it.

I went to work right away. The first night on the street I felt as if I was on display. You have to remember I hadn't been out hustling for a long time. I had to get used to it all over again.

And this time I was going to do it right. This time the money wasn't getting wasted. I would live good but I'd save my dough. I had to. I was almost thirty then. How many years were left? I'd need a little cushion when the fat years ran out, and there weren't many of them left for me. Not many at all.

I turned myself into a real working girl, believe me. I even opened a little savings account and put something into it every week. I've never taken it out and there's a few thousand in there already. It's insurance in several ways. If I ever do get busted again, I've got enough bread to make any cop in the world forget he ever saw me.

For a whore I'm a pretty respectable girl. The people In my building don't have any idea what I do for a living. I always come home from work with my face scrubbed and my clothes nice and neat. I don't have people over and I don't get stoned in my apartment. If I want to belt the bottle around or have myself a stick or two of pot, I use the place on 47th Street.

Respectable. Yeah, that's me, all right. But I don't feel so respectable. There's still four or five hours a day on the street or in the sack. There's still the way men look at me. One of these days my neighbor across the hall is going to run into me on

Seventh Avenue. It'll happen. And then I'll probably have to move. Respectable? Sure.

And it gets harder and harder to look in mirrors. Maybe I never should have gone on this respectable kick to begin with. It gets me seeing all the ways in which I'm not respectable at all. It's funny—the more I try to act like a human being, the more I see what a whore I am. I guess you just can't win. You can die trying, but you can't win.

Yesterday was a bad day. I got on the street a few minutes after twelve and nothing was happening. It was raining and tricks were scarce. A few guys passed, looking me over and then finding somebody else to go home with. I guess I don't look as good as I used to. There was a time when I would have been picked before anyone else on the street. But I guess those days are gone.

I went two hours without a nibble. It was getting bad. I stood by the Elpine fruit stand for a while and drank a few cups of lousy coffee, talking to the guy behind the counter. I leaned up against the walls of the Dale Dance Studio and said dirty things to the men as they passed. But nobody seemed to want me.

Then a man came along, short and mean-looking, one tooth broken off in front, blood in his eye. He wanted me. He would pay me. He would pay well—fifty dollars for a half-hour or so.

He wanted to beat me up.

He was honest at least. He told me just how far he would go. He said he could guarantee he wouldn't send me to a hospital and he wouldn't mark up my face. That's all he would guarantee. If I was game, fine. If I didn't want a beating he would go look for somebody else, somebody who didn't mind getting her lumps if she was making that kind of bread.

I told him no.

But it was a slow night and I had time to think about it. And I saw that there was going to be a day when I wouldn't turn him down, when I wouldn't turn anybody down, when I'd get my ribs kicked in for a few dollars if I had to.

I couldn't work any more when I thought like that. I caught a cab and went home to 73rd Street. I broke a rule by taking myself a few good slugs of gin. It helped, but not enough. I had to get out of the life. I had to straighten up and fly right, get out of New York and go to some little town somewhere where nobody would know what I was. I had the money, didn't I? Why didn't I go?

And that's the hell of it. I had the money but I knew damned well I wouldn't go. I don't know what it is that holds me here. Maybe a psychiatrist could tell me. I don't know.

The next night I was back on the street and I made over a hundred dollars in four hours flat.

If you're looking for an ending to this book you're in for a big disappointment. There isn't going to be any ending. It ends right where it started, with me on the street.

Some day there will be an ending.

I don't know how it'll come. Maybe one of these days I'll forget how scared I am of dying. Then I'll kill myself. I've thought about it a lot but I'm not sure exactly how I would do it. Sleeping pills is supposed to be the easiest way. You just take them and go to sleep and don't wake up. It sounds nice, sort of. I like sleeping.

Or maybe I'll drink so much that the liquor will get to me and I'll make an alcoholic scene. I hope not—just like I hope I won't wind up on junk. I might. My pot supplier can get hard stuff for me if I want it. God, I hope I don't go that way.

I probably won't. I've stayed away from it this long, just as I've stayed away from suicide and alcohol. I'll probably just keep on going. You know—old whores never die, they just fall apart.

You know where some of us wind up? On the Bowery. On Skid Row. Old and toothless, doing our work in an alley for fifty cents. You can't believe it? Well, it happens to be true.

Sixty years old and haggard and toothless and infected and rolling around like a pig with a drunk in an alley for enough money to buy a pint of sneaky Pete and . . .

God!

To hell with it. That's the story. Period. End of report. You want to know more, come on up for a personal interview. I'm not Mae West, but you can still come up and see me some time.

A Commentary

by Dr. Louis H. Gold

It isn't often that a psychiatrist has made available to him such a complete, firsthand report of the life of a person engaged in prostitution. When such a person is examined by court order she usually refrains from going into detail and is evasive. As one who has been connected with the courts for many years my reading the case history of Elizabeth Crowley was most illuminating and instructive. I will attempt to offer in simple terms an interpretation of her behavior and its meaning to society.

At the outset it should be stated that Elizabeth is a sick and tormented girl. Even though she may move freely within our community she is sick socially, morally and psychologically. The story she tells is one of painful human interest. It is in the rough and is close to the sidewalk. It is not a literary masterpiece but rather a poignant and frank description of a tortured soul severely traumatized in her early formative years, lacking in warm and satisfying human experiences, resorting to distorted and neurotic means of living and communicating with others. Elizabeth's behavior, although condemned and criticized by society in general, tells a story of discordant family relationships and takes on real meaning when one reads her history from a clinical view. It is adult material. Even a layman will agree that any child receiving such a poor start in life is as severely handicapped as one with a serious physical disease. In my estimation, as a physician who has been practicing psychiatry for almost thirty years and as a citizen, this case history deserves the intelligent understanding and concern of all of us.

Those who do not live in New York and are not familiar with the area described as Hell's Kitchen will find an accurate description of the neighborhood. It is a rough one. Women are afraid to walk in this region by themselves and I dare say that some men also feel uncomfortable and fear an assault if they have business in this district after dusk. There is nothing beautiful about the Kitchen. There was nothing beautiful in Elizabeth's home, or in her life.

Her mother's behavior resembled that of a sociopathic personality. There was practically no father. There was a lack of religious influence, there were no wholesome object identifications. There was no one in whom Elizabeth could take pride and with whom she could compare herself. The seeds of future disorder and disorganization were sown at an early age. Everything seemed to happen in a way that made for contempt and hostility. She visualized crude sexual activity in her home which was distasteful and frightening. She was attacked physically, and was raped at an early age.

There was very little to contribute to her own self-respect, to the formation of a sound system of values. The home was singularly free from discipline and guidance. Moral standards were absent except on rare occasions and then only feebly verbalized by the mother. From early life Elizabeth felt rejected and unwanted. While she never mentioned hating her mother, I am sure that there were deep mixed feelings toward her parent. In fact, most of Elizabeth's emotions were mixed and ambivalent. She never developed a sound image of herself, she never matured; her personality never developed concrete form. She was constantly torn by conflicting emotions. There was no opportunity to learn about wholesomeness except what her innate feelings suggested.

Her sexual experiences are vividly and pathetically described. There was no kindness, love, or decency to modify the sordidness of life. Her turning to prostitution is symbolic of a need, a compulsion to associate with someone, no matter the method, moral or risk. On the other hand her many conflicts and guilt feelings were always within her awareness. This will explain in part the mechanism of denial in most of her contacts. Actually, Elizabeth was a warm and loving person, endowed with the capacity to experience wholesome human relationships and emotions but unfortunately, because of deprivation, neglect, abandonment and horrible earlier traumatic experiences, her reactive behavior became distorted, corrupted and deviated. On occasion her trade reduced her identity almost to the primitive.

When one studies a life history such as herein described, he should understand the reasons for Elizabeth's deviation and be moved to ask "isn't there something that can be done about such cases?"

Some folks may exclaim "isn't this terrible!" Unfortunately, when the psychiatrist meets with such a problem he realizes that a great deal of injury has already occurred! Were it only possible to have removed Elizabeth from her home at birth and to have placed her in the hands of loving, yearning parents who would be able to supply her with the necessary spiritual, social and other healthy ego resources which are so vital to normal personality growth and development! I believe there will be universal agreement with the conclusion that trouble started in the home at birth and probably even earlier. You ask "what then can society do to prevent such sad situations from developing?" This is a complex question which has worried civilization for years. There is no simple solution. Much research is necessary. Books like these should remove the cloak of mystery and encourage public interest in this serious social problem.

Further analysis of this case history will reveal that Elizabeth's life was one of rebellion against society and its moral codes, rebellion against authority. This was her own way of life, of crying out. This was her peculiar compromise with society, her own personal philosophy. This kind of life is restricted, undesirable and regressive. People so afflicted are childish in many ways.

Page after page describes candid variations from normal activity. This is a striking and revealing sociological portrait without embellishments. Occasionally, there are moments when Elizabeth's remarks suggest introspection and sensitivity. Then there are moments of intense sadomasochism. Her appreciation of small favors is puerile. Even her reaction to guilt is childish and meaningless. Her long experience with psychological trauma has left little room for normal and tender human emotions. Bits of moral code are readily exhausted. Vulgarity and profanity become substitutes for language. Her course is steadily one of increasing deprivation, isolation and abandonment. Suicide is often contemplated and kept in reserve. She looks for a father, mother, for a friend, for love. These needs are never gratified. Fleeting associations are tenuously kept. Sincerity is an empty term. On one occasion she said "at first I did too much thinking and thinking is dangerous." Who is there who cannot feel compassion for Elizabeth?

Here is a small informative book with a rather provocative title! Between its covers lies an almost unbelievable tale of human bondage. Society needs to know more about the whole course of such misused lives before it can be awakened to support the research and education which this intense social problem demands.

Dr. Louis H. Gold

NOTE:

Dr. Louis H. Gold has been practicing psychiatry in Hartford, Connecticut for many years. He was graduated from New York Medical College in 1932, is a Fellow of The American Academy of Forensic Sciences and the American Psychiatric Association. He was President of the Medical Staff of the Mt. Sinai Hospital (Hartford) where he continues to serve as attending neuropsychiatrist. He was formerly Director of Neuropsychiatry at Rocky Hill Veteran's and McCook Memorial Hospitals.

He is on the psychiatric staff of the Hartford Police Court, was also psychiatrist to the Juvenile Court. He is consultant to The State Board of Education, is certified by The American Board of Psychiatry and Neurology.

My Newsletter: I get out an email newsletter at unpredictable intervals, but rarely more often than every other week. I'll be happy to add you to the distribution list. A blank email to lawbloc@gmail.com with "newsletter" in the subject line will get you on the list, and a click of the "Unsubscribe" link will get you off it, should you ultimately decide you're happier without it.

Lawrence Block has been writing award-winning mystery and suspense fiction for half a century. You can read his thoughts about crime fiction and crime writers in *The Crime of Our Lives*, where this MWA Grand Master tells it straight. His most recent novels are *The Girl With the Deep Blue Eyes*; *The Burglar Who Counted the Spoons*, featuring Bernie Rhodenbarr; *Hit Me,* featuring Keller; and *A Drop of the Hard Stuff,* featuring Matthew Scudder, played by Liam Neeson in the film *A Walk Among the Tombstones.* Several of his other books have been filmed, although not terribly well. He's well known for his books for writers, including the classic *Telling Lies for Fun &f Profit,* and *The Liar's Bible.* In addition to prose works, he has written episodic television (*Tilt!*) and the Wong Kar-wai film, *My Blueberry Nights.* He is a modest and humble fellow, although you would never guess as much from this biographical note.

Email: lawbloc@gmail.com
Twitter: @LawrenceBlock
Facebook: lawrence.block
Website: lawrenceblock.com

www.ingramcontent.com/pod-product-compliance
Lightning Source LLC
Chambersburg PA
CBHW070550180626
46817CB00005B/1774